"Look, Dr. Granger—"

"You can call me Jared."

Brooke caught his gaze. "No, I really can't. In order to maintain our professional arrangement, we need to keep this on a professional level."

"And that's not what we've been doing?"

"Well, yes. And no."

"Tell me about the no part."

She shrugged. "I've really enjoyed getting to know you better, but—well at times...." Her gaze faltered.

He leaned closer. "At times you felt something stirring between us?"

"Maybe. I don't know."

He released his breath on a sigh. "You're a very attractive woman. And if we're going to spend time together, I'd rather that we be friends than enemies."

"Okay," she said. "As long as you remember who's the boss."

He grinned. "Hell, I knew that the day I met you. But you'll have to be patient with me. I'm usually in charge."

Dear Reader,

Ring in the New Year with the hottest new love stories from Silhouette Desire! *The Redemption of Jefferson Cade* by BJ James is our MAN OF THE MONTH. In this latest installment of MEN OF BELLE TERRE, the youngest Cade overcomes both external and internal obstacles to regain his lost love. And be sure to read the launch book in Desire's first yearlong continuity series, DYNASTIES: THE CONNELLYS. In *Tall, Dark & Royal*, bestselling author Leanne Banks introduces a prominent Chicago family linked to European royals.

Anne Marie Winston offers another winner with *Billionaire Bachelors: Ryan*, a BABY BANK story featuring twin babies. In *The Tycoon's Temptation* by Katherine Garbera, a jaded billionaire discovers the greater rewards of love, while Kristi Gold's *Dr. Dangerous* discovers he's addicted to a certain physical therapist's personal approach to healing in this launch book of Kristi's MARRYING AN M.D. miniseries. And Metsy Hingle bring us *Navy SEAL Dad*, a BACHELORS & BABIES story.

Start the year off right by savoring all six of these passionate, powerful and provocative romances from Silhouette Desire!

Enjoy!

Joan Marlow Golan

Joan Marlow Golan
Senior Editor, Silhouette Desire

Please address questions and book requests to:
Silhouette Reader Service
U.S.: 3010 Walden Ave., P.O. Box 1325, Buffalo, NY 14269
Canadian: P.O. Box 609, Fort Erie, Ont. L2A 5X3

Dr. Dangerous
KRISTI GOLD

Published by Silhouette Books
America's Publisher of Contemporary Romance

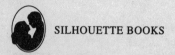 SILHOUETTE BOOKS

ISBN 0-373-76415-4

DR. DANGEROUS

Copyright © 2002 by Kristi Goldberg

This edition published by arrangement with Harlequin Books S.A.

® and TM are trademarks of Harlequin Books S.A., used under license. Trademarks indicated with ® are registered in the United States Patent and Trademark Office, the Canadian Trade Marks Office and in other countries.

Visit Silhouette at www.eHarlequin.com

Printed in U.S.A.

Books by Kristi Gold

Silhouette Desire

Cowboy for Keeps #1308
Doctor for Keeps #1320
His Sheltering Arms #1350
Her Ardent Sheikh #1358
*Dr. Dangerous #1415

*Marrying an M.D.

KRISTI GOLD

began her romance-writing career at the tender age of twelve, when she and her sister spun romantic yarns involving a childhood friend and a popular talk-show host. Since that time, she's given up celebrity heroes for her favorite types of men, doctors and cowboys, as her husband is both. An avid sports fan, she attends football and baseball games in her spare time. She resides on a small ranch in central Texas with her three children and retired neurosurgeon husband, along with various livestock ranging from Texas longhorn cattle to spoiled yet talented equines. At one time she competed in regional and national Appaloosa horse shows as a non-pro, but she gave up riding for writing and turned the "reins" over to her youngest daughter. She attributes much of her success to her sister, Kim, who encouraged her in her writing, even during the tough times. When she's not in her office writing her current book, she's dreaming about it. Readers may contact Kristi at P.O. Box 11292, Robinson, TX 76116.

To my husband, Steve,
who has shown me the true and loving heart of a healer

One

Administering physical therapy had always been a challenge Brooke Lewis readily embraced, but the anger in her new patient's you-want-me blue eyes and the defiance in his here-I-am stance, made her want to run for the nearest fast-food joint for employment. Or to her boss, Macy Carpenter, armed with a noose.

Dr. Jared Granger, "King of Cardiology"—the man she had shamelessly fantasized about from afar—had graced her with his presence. And not one solitary soul in the department had bothered to warn her.

Many times she'd admired him as he strode through San Antonio Memorial's corridors in his impeccably starched lab coat, wearing his gorgeous golden hair, cut in the latest style, and a guarded expression that discouraged any kind of communication.

It came with the territory, she supposed. Anyone who held life in his hands on a daily basis wasn't necessarily approachable.

But since the recent injury that had suspended his career, he had obviously changed. Now his sandy hair was askew, and his normally clean-shaven face sported a near-full beard. His ragged jeans with one leg cut away revealed a cast on his left leg. Overall, his attire looked as though it had seen better days. But then, so did he. From all appearances he could be a drifter, not a doctor.

And for the past few weeks his uncooperative behavior had grown to legendary proportions in the physical therapy department. Brooke had managed to avoid his wrath. Until now.

Not to mention she would have to touch him, and although that certainly wasn't an unpleasant prospect under normal circumstances, she had the distinct feeling he wasn't going to be too receptive.

She opened her mouth, but words didn't form. Nothing seemed quite adequate at the moment.

Smiling, she gestured toward the chair facing hers. "Nice you could join us today, Dr. Granger. Please be seated."

Without speaking, he hobbled over with his lone crutch and sank into the chair, sprawling his broken leg awkwardly to one side as he propped his splinted hand on the small table's surface in arm-wrestling position. She pulled the curtain around the area to give them some privacy, away from the prying eyes of both patients and therapists throughout the large treatment room.

When Brooke faced him, he flashed her a sardonic grin. "So you're my next victim."

The impact of that smile, no matter how cynical, did things to her heart rate that made her wonder if she needed a round of digitalis. Thank heavens she was close to the chair before her knees gave way. After taking her seat across from him, she said, "Victim? That should be my line."

Brooke opened the chart to review the assessment and treatment plan along with the notes of his limited progress. Victim proved to be an appropriate description. He'd already been through three therapists in three weeks, and it looked as if she was his last resort.

Glancing up, Brooke found him staring at her, watching, waiting. Waiting for her to screw up, she decided. But his visual assessment made her wonder if that was all he was waiting for. Considering his reputation with women, he probably expected her to pass out from a charisma overdose. Well, he had another thing coming. She'd keep her covert admiration to herself and a tight rein on her hormones.

With a polite smile she closed the chart and set it on the end of the table. "I'm Brooke Lewis, and it looks like we'll be working together for some time, Dr. Gran—"

"Don't count on it." He displayed more insolence through the hard set of his eyes and the tight ridge of his jaw.

Good Lord, she wanted to scream all of two minutes into the appointment. "I don't understand. Dr. Kempner wants extensive therapy treatments for your hand."

"Yeah, that's what he wants."

"And you don't want that?"

"I hate this whole process."

Brooke got the distinct feeling she would, too, before it was all over. "Well, let's see if we can make this as pleasant as possible for both of us. If you're going to return to surgery, then—"

"I don't want that mentioned again. Ever."

He sat forward, skewering her with his unwavering gaze, giving her a good dose of his pain. Not physical pain. She could handle that. It was her job to make it all better, and sometimes that meant making a patient physically hurt from the effort. But emotional pain... That was another thing altogether. She was a sucker for sympathy, and right now she didn't want to be sympathetic to a God complex in action. But she was. It went beyond his looks. His aura of power. He couldn't mask the frustration in his eyes, those windows to the soul that Brooke had learned to look through to find the person beneath the facade. And this particular person was totally torn up inside.

Straightening her spine, Brooke tried to affect her usual cheerful disposition. "Okay, so we'll work on stretching those tendons, and then we'll see what's what." She reached for his hand to remove the splint, but he pulled away.

"I'll do it." With slow, stilted movements, he took off the splint while Brooke waited patiently. At least this was a positive sign, wanting to do it himself. Some of his pride was still intact. And that could mean more grief for her.

While Brooke allowed him this act of independence, she considered his predicament. A doctor who had lost the function of his dominant hand—his instrument of healing. A skilled surgeon who could very well find himself without a career if he didn't mend.

He had the right to be a little ticked off. Anger was sometimes a good thing. A great motivator. Considering the fact that during the accident he'd damaged the flexor tendons in three of his fingers, he needed some motivation for the long haul to recovery. The question was, would Brooke be up to it? *If* he didn't fire her first.

Gently she took his hand into hers. His fingers were large, well-defined, yet rigid because of the accident. "Have you been doing your passive motion protocol at home?"

He shrugged and looked away. "When I find the time."

Oh, boy. He was going to test her to the max.

Brooke conducted a visual search and homed in on his wrist. The dense scar, to say the least, was ugly. She touched it, and he flinched. "Still ultrasensitive there, I take it."

"No kidding."

Ignoring his sarcasm, she examined his thumb. "Do you feel that?"

"No."

She moved on to his pointer finger. "Here?"

He pulled his hand away quickly, startling Brooke. "Look, I've already been through this," he said, fire and frustration in his tone. "I've got no sensitivity on the volar surface of my thumb, no feeling on the second finger and diminished sensitivity on the third. My tendons are a bloody mess, and a whole army of therapists can't do a damn thing about it."

Brooke put on her calm face and waited to see if he was finished with his outburst. When he seemed to relax somewhat, she forced another smile and spoke through it. "Dr. Granger, I realize that you probably know as much if not more than me about your condition. I know this is a horribly painful thing to go through. I also know that if you don't opt to continue therapy, you might never be able to pick up anything smaller than an orange, much less a scalpel."

She stared at him straight on, surprised he had yet to protest since she'd mentioned another *S* word. When he didn't respond, she continued. "So if you're willing to cooperate, then I'll do my best to assist you. But I can't do this alone."

"And I can't do this at all."

Brooke expected him to vault out of the chair and head out the door, but he didn't. What was holding him here, if he was so bent on nixing therapy? Why was he wasting her time? Anyone's time, for that matter?

That wasn't relevant. It was her job to put him through the motions. Her job to see to it that he at least attempted to accomplish something. Her job to hang on to her cool.

While Brooke applied moist heat to his wrist as well as electronic stimulation to try and alleviate some of the scar tissue, he didn't say a word. She administered myofacial massage and stretching exercises to relax his tendons, and still he didn't speak. In fact, he didn't react at all except to flinch now and then. Even when she tried to engage him in mundane conversation about the unseasonable weather, he replied in one-word responses. She might as well talk to the wall.

"Okay, time for something new," she said, trying to spark his enthusiasm. His posture wasn't the greatest, but she thought it best not to scold him too much. "Just sit up a little straighter and we'll try this for a minute."

He moved maybe a microinch. She put the small red foam ball in his palm. "Can you try to grip this?" she asked.

After staring at the ball like it was some alien entity, he let it slip from his grasp without even trying. It rolled onto the floor beside the table. Brooke quietly retrieved it, barely avoiding knocking her toe on his cast. Again she placed the ball in his palm. Again it rolled away, this time under the table before Brooke could thwart its escape.

Drawing in a cleansing breath, she leaned down and felt around for the offending object. Not finding it, she bent farther underneath the table, grabbed up the ball, and promptly bumped her head on the edge when she straightened.

She rose and found the not-so-good doctor staring off into space. Obviously her near concussion meant nothing to him. Not even worth a "Is your head okay?" or "Hope you didn't break the table." Just absolute detachment, as if he wanted to be somewhere else. Anywhere else. At the moment so did she.

When Brooke awakened that morning to the first cold front of the season mixed with bone-biting rain, the second flat tire in a week and a dead coffeemaker, she'd been primed for a typical Monday. But she didn't deserve this, even from the man who had once been the doctor of her dreams.

Anger began to seep into Brooke's pores. No matter how hard she tried to plug up the hole in her resolve so the frustration wouldn't escape, another fissure took its place. She was known for tolerating difficult patients. Known to never lose her composure. But today had been the mother of all bad days, and right now she was feeling anything but composed. What else would explain the sudden need to respond to his apathy with a curtness totally foreign to her?

Brooke choked the ball in her fist and leveled her gaze on him. "*Dr.* Granger, since you seem to be having a problem with cooperation, it just occurred to me that maybe you're having a temporary bout of self-pity. At least, I hope it's only temporary, because if you want to see something to feel sorry for, then hang around for my next patient. A twenty-five-year-old father of two with a fractured C-6 vertebrae.''

She paused only long enough to take a deep draw of air. "He comes here in a wheelchair with his kids on his lap and a smile on his face even though he'll never take another step. Never make another baby. Never even make love to his wife in the same way again. But he's not moaning over his situation. He's going about the business of living, even though he has little opportunity to get better. You do.''

For a moment he looked as though she had struck him. He opened his mouth, then let it drop shut. Awkwardly he stood, looming over her like a sturdy oak able to survive the greatest of storms, his face flashing anger. But his eyes looked vulnerable. So very, very vulnerable.

"I don't need your lecture, Ms. Lewis. I've spent the last eight years of my life operating on sick people, many of them kids, and with every one that I lost, part of me died right with them. But I kept going because I couldn't do anything but be a doctor. I didn't *want* to be anything but a doctor. I still don't."

He held up his stiff right hand. It trembled like a fragile leaf. "If you take away this, you might as well take away my legs, too."

With that, he pivoted around and tore back the curtain. And Brooke immediately experienced the biting pang of remorse. She'd forced him to bare his soul. Forced him to uncover a wound that was forty times the size of his scar.

Brooke rose on shaky legs, afraid that she had totally turned him off to therapy—totally blown his world apart with her callous behavior. And in the process, she could have jeopardized her job, the most worthwhile thing in her life. But more important, she had kicked a man at his lowest point—a talented doctor whose potential was limitless and, because of one life-altering accident, was now nothing more than the shell of the man he used to be. Regardless of his bitter attitude, that was unforgivable.

"Dr. Granger, wait," she called out before he reached the door. Several therapists stopped their own activities and briefly gave their attention to Brooke.

Dr. Granger halted and turned. This time his eyes looked lifeless. Dead. And something deep inside Brooke died, too.

She joined him at the doorway and signaled him to follow her into the hall. Once there, she lowered her eyes because it was simply too painful to look at him.

"I'm sorry. I didn't mean to come down on you so hard. It's just that if you give up, it would be such a waste."

"Would it?"

She looked up to find him studying her, this time with a penetrating sadness that cut to the heart. "A terrible waste. I propose you come back on Thursday, and we'll start over again."

"I hate coming here."

"I know, but once you settle into the routine, it will get easier."

"Not here, with you. Here, in the hospital."

His hospital, Brooke thought. A place that had been a huge part of his life. A place full of reminders of what he'd once had—a brilliant career.

Brooke certainly couldn't blame him for being less than thrilled to return on a regular basis. She also couldn't allow him to fall into complacency. Yet she wasn't sure how to convince him that he needed to continue the therapy if he was frustrated by the hospital surroundings.

A sudden thought crossed her mind. A crazy thought, but just crazy enough to work.

"Dr. Granger, have you considered home therapy?"

His eyes narrowed. "You mean someone coming to my house instead of me coming here?"

"Yeah. It's been done before." Brooke had done it before, mostly with shut-ins. Never with a struggling, handsome doctor.

"You'd be willing to come to my home?" he asked, surprise in his tone.

"Well, yes. Or someone else, if you prefer."

"No. I'd want it to be you."

He seemed so adamant that she continue his therapy, Brooke was almost rendered speechless. "So you'd consider it?"

"Maybe."

Brooke released the breath she'd been holding. "I'll have to clear it with my supervisor, and we'll need to talk with Dr. Kempner about changing the order."

"He'll do it."

"So you'll think about it?"

"We'll see." He limped down the corridor with a slump to his shoulders, all the pride seeming to have seeped from him in a matter of moments.

Somehow, some way, Brooke was determined to set things right, and if he agreed to the home therapy, that was a start.

If he allowed her the opportunity to aid in his recovery, hopefully when the time came, she would walk away from him knowing that she had helped him in some small way. Walk away and never look back. But deep down, Brooke worried that walking away from Jared Granger might be easier planned than done, especially if he didn't get better.

Yet she *had* to walk away, and without any second thoughts. Becoming emotionally involved with a patient was not only taboo, but created a danger to Brooke's emotional well-being. Leaving her heart wide open was not an option.

Yes, Dr. Jared Granger might need her, but she would never need another man again.

Jared Granger waited alone in Nick Kempner's office, studying his rigid hand, his gnarled fingers. He hated sympathy of any kind, the pitying looks he received from colleagues and friends alike. Hated the fact that he was steeped in self-pity more often than not these days.

Never had he been posed with such a challenge. Even med school and multiple residencies hadn't gotten him down like this. Might as well admit it, he was washed up as a surgeon. Not much better off as a man. At least not at the present.

Admitting it didn't take away the pain, the anger. It only served to create more vile-tasting resentment that he couldn't control.

He also couldn't recall the last good day he'd had, even before the accident. Three weeks ago, getting away to his farm—a place he could always count on to regroup—hadn't eased the piercing guilt over losing a special patient, the reason why he hadn't been paying attention to the thin piece of wire caught in the tractor shredder. The reason he'd carelessly tried to manhandle it out of the blade, causing the backlash that had sent the metal slicing across his wrist, creating the deep laceration that damaged his median nerve, then the fall that had shattered his leg. All in a few short moments of stupidity, he had ruined a career years in the making.

He recalled twelve-year-old Kayla Brown's death, why he'd gone to his weekend retreat in the first place. She'd been faced with rejection of her new heart and awaiting another when she'd finally given up after fighting the good fight. Jared hadn't been able to save the young girl who had been a natural room brightener. A kid who always smiled no matter how much pain she endured or how constant the prospect of death.

His problems were minor compared to what she had faced. So what if it took him an hour longer to brush his teeth, dress himself, pour a glass of milk? So what if he could barely manage to clean himself? He'd be damned and desperate before he would admit that to anyone. No one would understand.

Brooke Lewis immediately came to mind—her wild, dark curls, big brown eyes, natural smile and die-hard attitude. As badly as he hated to admit it, he admired her grit as much as he admired her schoolgirl looks. She didn't view him as anything other than a patient. He found that refreshing, since most people treated him as if he was some infallible being without a heart or feelings. No one knew the real Jared Granger, because he had never revealed much of himself; he feared that he could never live up to others' expectations.

The door swung open and Nick Kempner strode in, the best orthopedic doc in the business, and Jared's closest friend. "What's up, Granger?"

"Not much."

Nick slipped out of his lab coat and tossed it and several newspapers from his seat onto the nearby sofa before sinking into the office chair. "Sorry I'm late, but I had to take a call at the front desk."

"No problem." And it wasn't. Jared had nowhere to be at the moment. Nowhere to be most days in recent history, except doctor appointments and dreaded therapy sessions.

Nick folded his hands in front of him and brought

out his all-business face. "The call was from your latest therapist."

Jared braced for another lecture. "Yeah?"

"Yeah. She told me that although you were, and I quote 'a bit uncooperative,' she would work around it. She mentioned maybe home therapy. What do you think about that?"

The woman was as persistent as a moth on a porch light. "Therapy isn't doing me a helluva lot of good."

"That's because you're not giving it a chance."

"She looks too young to know what she's doing." And too pretty to ignore, as much as Jared hated to admit that.

"She's not a kid, Granger. She's got a master's degree, and she's been working here for several years. In fact, she's at least twenty-five. Probably older."

"In my book that's still a kid."

"To hear you talk, you're sixty, not thirty-six."

"I feel like I'm eighty."

Nick forked a hand through his dark hair. "Look, Brooke Lewis is one of the best therapists around. If you give her the opportunity, she can help you with those tendons. It's just going to take some time and hard work on your part."

If Jared could ball his fist, he'd punch the wall. He could do that with his left hand, but considering his recent misfortune, he'd probably ruin it, too. "What you're saying is that I might never operate again."

Nick let go a frustrated sigh. "Don't put words in my mouth, Jared. I'm saying you need to give the therapy a shot, and the best place to start is with Brooke." He grinned. "And you've got to admit, she's pretty nice to look at. Can't imagine you'd mind having her touching you twice a week—wherever she wanted.''

Jared refused to admit that the thought had crossed his mind, too. He'd immediately been aware of her finer points. When she'd touched him, his immediate reaction had taken him back, the reason why he'd been so tough on her. He didn't need an attraction to a woman, especially a therapist. Not that he could easily stop it. At least that part of him wasn't exactly dead. Not by a long shot. Brooke Lewis had proven that. But at the moment, he had other more pressing problems, like getting his hand to function again.

''If you think she's so great, then you make an appointment with her for some hands-on therapy,'' Jared said.

Nick shook his head. ''No way. I've sworn off women since the divorce.''

''Sure, Kempner. Tell me another one.''

''I'm dead serious. Not worth the hassle.''

''Speaking of women, how's it going with your ex?''

Nick grabbed up a pen and drummed it on the desktop. ''Not great. I only have to see her when I pick up Kelsey on the weekends that I'm not on call. We barely speak, which is probably a good thing. Fighting in front of a four-year-old isn't a great idea.''

Jared hated the pain in his friend's voice. Pain over limited time with his daughter all because of marrying the wrong woman. But how could anyone know if they'd found the right one?

Nick had a point, Jared decided. Sometimes women weren't worth the hassle. Marriage definitely wasn't, exactly why Jared had avoided it, especially with the demands of a doctor's career. Not that he'd had to worry about that lately.

Nick tossed the pen aside and leaned back in his chair. "Jared, I know you're having a tough time with this whole thing. If you want someone to talk to, I have the name of—"

"I'm not depressed, dammit. I'm just ticked off." God, he resented this attitude. Resented that people were always trying to second-guess his feelings, when in reality they didn't know him at all.

Nick put up his hands, palms first. "Okay, bad idea. But I really think you need to concentrate on physical therapy. You could do a lot worse than Brooke Lewis."

He could do a lot better if he could just crawl in a hole somewhere and lick his wounds. But that wasn't reality. He had to deal with this somehow. And maybe the hell-on-wheels therapist with the killer smile and dynamite eyes was the answer, at least temporarily. Maybe Brooke Lewis's offer wasn't such a bad idea.

Jared stared at the ceiling for a long moment, sensing Nick's gaze on him while awaiting an answer. "Okay. Set up the home therapy. I'm not making any promises, but I guess I'll take on Brooke Lewis."

Nick laughed. "I think that's the other way around."

If his instincts were correct, Jared knew in his gut that working with Brooke Lewis could be like facing a pit full of vipers. But before the accident he'd never backed down to a challenge. Not true since the accident, though. Could he handle this one, especially with a woman who had sparked his interest, among other things? Did he really have a choice?

"One more thing," Nick said. "She told me that next time you can count on her to use putty to work your hand instead of the ball, since it doesn't bounce. Any idea what that means?"

Jared allowed his first real smile in weeks. "Yeah, it means I've probably met my match."

Two

"**R**ural" was an understatement.

Brooke climbed out of her car and trudged toward the door after driving an hour in the dark to reach her destination. She'd checked the address at the mailbox just to be sure she was in the right place. And she was, but the place wasn't at all what she had envisioned—a small white house that could use a good coat of paint as best she could tell from the lone porch light. A simple dwelling to match the aged blue pickup that sat in the drive and the weathered plank porch beneath her feet.

She'd imagined a grand home fit for a physician, not a cracker box dwelling that reminded her of her grandparent's farm. Once again Dr. Jared Granger had surprised her, and she wondered what else might be in store for her this evening.

But at least he had agreed to home therapy, something that both surprised and pleased her. And made her a tiny bit leery. Facing him in unfamiliar surroundings—his territory—caused her to question the wisdom of her offer. She certainly couldn't worry about that now.

Brooke bolstered her courage and rapped on the door, primed for whatever she would have to face. She waited for a time, glad the weather had turned warm again, although it still rained on and off. So typical of fall in Texas.

She heard a shuffling sound, and the door opened to Dr. Jared Granger dressed in ragged T-shirt, faded jeans, his dark-blond hair mussed as if he'd just crawled out of bed.

"You found me," he said with more welcome in his tone than she'd expected. Or perhaps she was simply engaging in wishful thinking.

"Yeah," she said. "Dr. Kempner gives good directions."

He opened the squeaky screen and allowed her entry. Brooke stepped inside and found the place to be warm and dry—and a total disaster. Her gaze roamed around the small living room where she zeroed in on the coffee table cluttered with newspapers and an assortment of paper cups. A pair of discarded work boots sat near an opening at one end of the room, clothes tossed about as if a tornado had swept through the area. Several times. Quite a contrast to her immaculate apartment.

Taking a few guarded steps, Brooke met his gaze and offered a polite, noncommittal smile. "Well, this is certainly a comfortable home."

He shrugged. "Suits me fine."

She shifted her canvas bag from one arm to the other. "Where would you like me to set up?"

"In here." He leaned heavily on his crutch as he struggled toward the entrance that opened into the small kitchen.

Brooke followed silently behind him, trying hard not to notice the tear beneath his back pocket where she caught a glimpse of flesh when he moved. No need to look there again, but she couldn't seem to help herself.

Once in the kitchen Brooke found more mess to garner her attention. More discarded food containers, more newspapers, more chaos.

He pointed to the small dinette. "Will this work?"

She couldn't see anything at all because of the debris. "Is there a table under there?"

"Yeah. Somewhere."

He looked up at her, and she noted a bit of self-consciousness in his expression. With one arm braced on his crutch, he began to sweep the mess away with his free forearm, onto chairs, the floor, wherever it happened to land. If only Brooke's mother could witness this act. She'd faint.

"Look," Brooke said. "Find a chair, have a seat, and let me pick up some of this."

He pinned her with an irritated glare. "I didn't hire you to be my maid."

"And I didn't sign on to be one. But if we're going to make any progress, I need some room. It'll only take a minute if you'll point me to the trash bags."

He indicated a cabinet underneath the sink. "Right there. If you insist."

"I insist." Setting her tote bag on the hardwood floor, she made her way to the cabinet and opened the door to find an overflowing trashcan. "You've obviously given your housekeeper the year off."

"She's at my house in town."

She regarded him over one shoulder. "You have a house in town? Then why aren't you living there?"

"I like it here. More secluded."

"You can say that again," Brooke muttered as she bent over to tug a black bag from the cardboard dispenser. She turned to face him and shook the bag out, surprised to find an indescribable darkness in his normally light eyes. "Maybe you could get your housekeeper out here for some spring cleaning."

"It's fall, and I don't want her here." His tone was harsh, and Brooke got the feeling he didn't want her there, either. Back to square one.

His resistance only fueled her tenacity. Made her want to try a little harder to gain his respect, or at least his cooperation. "Well, I'm no domestic goddess, but I can handle the trash." Her mother fit the prima housekeeper role perfectly, and there was only room for one of those in the family. Neither she nor her sister, Michelle, had ever embraced domestic bliss. Right now she had little choice in the matter.

Brooke stared at the pile of dirty dishes in the sink and wondered how long they'd been there. A long time from the looks of the caked-on food, at least since the accident. Turning back to the table, she began slipping cartons of every shape and size, paper cups, a few discarded newspapers and myriad pizza boxes, into the bag.

After that was done, and she could actually see the

scuffed wooden table, she gathered up her bag, took out her pen and forms to note his progress and sat facing him. "Have you started doing your home therapy as prescribed?"

"Some."

She looked up from her charting. "Explain 'some.'"

He struggled to remove the splint, avoiding her gaze. "Once since last week."

She jotted the note and tamped down her frustration. "You might want to try at least once a day. Twice or three times would be better."

"Yeah, well, I don't have the energy. By the time I get up in the morning, try to clean up, then get dressed, I've wasted half the damned day, and all I want to do is take a nap."

Little did he know, Brooke could relate to that. If she had a particularly rough asthma attack, her weakness sometimes slowed her to a snail's pace.

"Okay. Now let's get down to business." She looked toward the mound cluttering the sink. How could she run water if she couldn't find the faucet? How could she heat water if she couldn't find a clean pot to boil the packs? Heaven help her, she would have to wash dishes, or at least try to clear some of them away. Her mother would be so proud.

Without speaking, Brooke rose and began stacking some glasses to one side of the sink until she had a makeshift fortress teetering on the edge of catastrophe. Finally she made enough room to draw some water. Now, to find some kind of soap.

Bending down, she retrieved a half-full bottle of dishwashing liquid from the cabinet underneath and squirted a few drops into the sink. She washed the pot with the least dried on food, filled it with water, dropped the pack in, then set it on the gas stove to heat.

While waiting for the water to boil, she went back to the sink and the Mt. Everest mess. After remarkably finding a clean towel and rag in the drawer, she dove into the task of dishwashing, her back to him while he waited at the table.

The silence was almost as stifling as the unpleasant odor wafting from the dirty dishes. She struggled for something to say to break the awkwardness. "Looks like you've gotten to know every pizza deliveryman in the county. Pepperoni or the works?" She smiled over one shoulder and found him staring at her, his blue eyes sharp and intense.

"Neither. Just the plain stuff for me."

"Really? I wouldn't have guessed that."

"Why?"

"It's that whole doctor persona. I've always believed that most medical men have a predilection for the exotic. You know, fast cars. Faster women."

"That's the problem with stereotypes. People get too bogged down in them."

She rimmed one glass with the cloth, over and over, until it squeaked. "So that's not the case with you?"

"Depends. Which one are you referring to? Cars, pizza or women?"

Boy, oh, boy, did she want to know about the latter. Why, she couldn't say. But she did. "All of the above."

"I like my old truck, which on a warm day can

actually top fifty-five if I get a running start. I like my pizza with double cheese and sometimes sausage. And what was that last one?'' he asked, amusement in his tone.

''Women.''

A chuckle rumbled low in his chest, lifting Brooke's spirits a notch. ''I like to know that they don't have to have a running start to reach the speed limit, and covered in cheese is just fine by me.''

My goodness. The doctor had a sense of humor. And she had a bad case of pleasant chills. ''Well, those are certainly impeccable standards.''

''What about you? What are your requirements in a man?''

''A man?'' She sounded as though she didn't know the meaning of the word.

''Yeah. What's your boyfriend like?''

She released a sharp humorless laugh. ''Nonexistent.''

''I'm surprised. Seems to me a woman as attractive as you would have a significant other.''

The glass she'd been washing for a ridiculous amount of time slipped from her grasp and fell back into the sink, sending a fountain of water onto the front of her lab coat. She ignored the dampness but couldn't seem to ignore his compliment or her pulse's pitter-patter rhythm. Yet she had to if she wanted to keep her head on straight. ''Nope, no significant other. I don't really have the inclination at this point in my career.'' Or the strength of will to investigate that possibility. Not after her one terrible experience with a man who'd used her, then discarded as easily as she'd just discarded the trash in Jared Granger's kitchen.

"Your career is the most important thing to you." He posed it as a straightforward statement of fact, not a question.

"Yes, you could say that. One day I plan to start my own clinic."

The chair creaked behind her, indicating he shifted in his seat. "So you have it all mapped out, huh? How long it will take to reach this goal, then the next, until it all comes together. Then the next thing you know, everything's on course, just the way you planned it, not believing for a minute it can all come apart at the seams in a matter of moments."

Setting the last of the glasses aside, she faced him, knowing he spoke of his own life as much as he spoke of hers. "Sure. But I guess nothing's guaranteed, right?"

"Yeah. And that's a damned bitter pill to swallow."

The familiar pain slid across his taut features once again. Brooke held on tightly to a thin rein of control. She couldn't keep playing into the sympathy. She needed to stay focused. Remain objective.

She retrieved the hot pack, wrapped it in another dish towel and applied it to his hand before going back to the dishes. She finished her chores while the allotted twenty minutes passed, enough time for the heat to relax his tendons, and all the excuse she needed to get back to the business at hand—helping him put his life back on track.

"Did washing my dirty dishes give you some kind

of thrill?" he asked as she took his hand into hers to begin the therapy.

She stared up at him, surprised to find amusement in his eyes. "Nope, just dishpan hands. Why?"

"You were whistling, like you really enjoyed it."

If the truth were known, it had given her a little boost. Because of her mother's penchant for cleaning on a weekly basis to prevent aggravating Brooke's asthma, she rarely did anything in the way of housekeeping, and she kind of liked the independence of not having someone standing over her shoulder, telling her she wasn't doing it right. Not that she'd reveal that to the physician. She didn't want him to erroneously assume that cleaning up after him would be a common occurrence. She hadn't enjoyed it *that* much. And it wasn't in her job description, either.

"Believe me, Dr. Granger," she said, "I'll send you a bill for my KP duties."

"No problem."

She looked up from working his fingers and met his compelling blue eyes once again. "How much do you think I should charge?"

"Whatever's fair."

"How much do you charge for, let's say, a quadruple bypass?"

He smiled again, but only part way. "Are you making a comparison here?"

"I think it's only fair, don't you? It took me over a half hour to consult with your dishes."

"At least they didn't talk back. And they sure as hell can't sue you if you happen to break one."

Another glimpse of wry humor. "Good point," she said, pleased by the fact that his tension over her presence had seemed to ease. Unfortunately, she couldn't say the same for his stiff, injured fingers, especially his pointer finger. She had her suspicions what the problem could be.

She curled her own fingers into his palm. "Can you grip my hand?"

With his brows drawn down in concentration, he moved his appendages somewhat. Not much, but enough to heighten Brooke's optimism. And heighten her awareness of the size of his hand. Hers looked small resting in the well of his large palm. Vulnerable. She could imagine how skilled his hand once was, in various undertakings that had nothing to do with surgery.

"Great," she said, pulling her hand away, pushing the questionable thoughts from her brain. "You need to really tackle the home therapy more often. Your second digit is the worst, and I'd hate to think you might develop a contracture."

He frowned. "You really think that's going to happen?"

"Hopefully not, but that's why you need to really work hard so we can prevent that from happening."

"I'll try."

At least that was some semblance of a commitment, Brooke decided.

After Brooke finished the treatment, she checked the clock again. More than an hour had passed, and she was beat.

"All done here," she said after putting away her equipment. "Guess I'd better go."

"One other thing," he said. "A favor, really." He looked as if it was costing him a lot to ask.

"What favor?"

"I'm having trouble doing some things. Personal things."

Whoa, Nelly. Brooke wasn't at all sure what he meant by that, or if she even wanted to know. Or did she? "What kinds of things?"

He rubbed his bearded chin. "Shaving, for one."

A doctor who performed open-heart surgery on a regular basis had just admitted that he had trouble using a razor. The old sympathy bug bit into Brooke once again. She tried to resist its sting. "Have you thought about hiring an occupational therapist or maybe a home healthcare aide?"

"I don't want to involve anyone else."

She could understand that he wanted to maintain as much privacy as possible, but where did she fit into this picture? "I'm not sure I can help you."

"I assume you know something about OT."

"Yes. Some."

"Then I don't see why you can't do it. I'll make sure you receive extra pay for your time. We could make it a private arrangement."

It wasn't the money that concerned Brooke, not that she couldn't use the extra funds. The fact that she would be even more deeply involved in his recovery, his life, bothered her on some level she didn't care to explore at the moment.

Her mind catalogued all the pros and cons. The pros won out. She was going to do it. Help him with personal things. And of course, administer therapy.

"Okay, I can help you shave. Shouldn't be too difficult."

His expression suddenly turned serious. "First, there's something I need to say."

Brooke braced for a demand, a warning, something in his tone that would help her regain her emotional bearings.

"I just wanted to say thanks," he said. "It's been a long time since..." He studied the table before looking up again. "Not many people would be willing to do this for me. I appreciate it."

She smiled, buoyed by his gratitude. "You're welcome. So do you want to try the shaving tonight?"

"Yeah, if you don't mind." He rubbed a hand over his almost full beard. "I thought it would be easy to do with my left hand, but it's weird how you take things for granted, like how you need fingers to lift your nose up to get to your upper lip."

"To be honest, I've never thought about it." She stood. "You want to do it here or in the bathroom?"

His smile came slowly, a hint of devilment in his crystalline eyes. "Where do you like to do it?"

Brooke's face heated to desert proportions. Had he really sounded that suggestive? Or was she simply imagining the innuendo? "Depends. How small is your bathroom?"

"Not nearly big enough, unless we stand up. I might have a hard time maneuvering with my bum leg." His eyes sparkled in the overhead light, full of mischief and something else. Surely not desire, Brooke thought.

Another image filtered into Brooke's brain, this one much more vivid. A vision of heated kisses, his hands on her, his mouth on her...

Obviously her libido had suddenly commandeered her brain.

Get a grip, Brooke. "I think that since you're fairly tall, in order for me to show you how to hold the razor, you should be sitting, and I should be standing. Don't you agree?"

"Oh, so we're back to shaving again."

"I don't think we ever really left. Did we?" She cringed at the question, as if she were baiting him to admit that for a moment he was considering other things, too.

"I don't know about you," he said with a wicked smile, "but I just took a mental trip that didn't have a damn thing to do with personal hygiene."

Surely he wasn't already suffering from transference, that pesky condition where a patient thought himself in love with his therapist. No, she didn't think so. Besides, this had more to do with lust, not love, although that wasn't totally out of the ordinary, either. He was simply trying to validate himself as a man. Needing some confirmation was understandable. And for heaven's sake, she'd only touched his hand up to this point. But she was about to touch his face. Much more intimate, and not a repulsive idea at all.

Stiffening her frame, she forced herself into business mode. "You just stay where you are. We can do it…shave you in here." She looked around the room. "I'll need an outlet for your razor."

"I don't use an electric razor. I prefer a blade."

Wonderful. "Maybe you should reconsider, at least until your hand's better."

"I like using the real thing, so you're not going to

get me to bend on this one. Besides, most women prefer a closer shave. Less whisker burn. Don't you?''

He was doing it again, making her feel all hot and bothered. And those darned scenarios that kept popping into her brain. The man had more pull than a Supreme Court judge. No wonder he was also known as the Stud of Surgery. "Okay, we'll work around it. Where are some scissors? I need to cut off the excess fur before we bring out the razor.''

"In the bathroom drawer,'' he said, pointing toward the hallway leading from the living room. "First door on the right. Shaving cream's in the medicine cabinet along with the razor.''

Making her way down the hardwood hallway floor, Brooke came to the small bathroom. It, too, was cluttered with towels and discarded rags piled in the corner.

She rummaged through the organized drawer and found the scissors with little trouble. The mirrored medicine cabinet was much the same, everything lined up in neat rows like multicolored perennials in an immaculate garden. Obviously he'd had some order in his life at one time.

She opened the linen closet behind her. It was bare. No towels, no washcloths. He must be recycling, but for how long? She couldn't tolerate the thought of many weeks worth of used towels. Only one option remained. She'd have to do laundry. Her mother would be doubly proud.

Gathering up a load of towels in her arms, the shaving cream, razor and scissors tucked in her lab coat pocket, Brooke headed back into the kitchen. "I thought I'd throw a load of towels in—'' She halted in midstride and midsentence when she came upon the doctor, sitting at the table, sans shirt.

Her gaze roamed over his bared chest covered by a spattering of golden hair. A well-defined road map to a prime physique. His belly was flat, revealing a nice six-pack of muscle, and she wondered how the heck he'd been lifting weights with one bad hand and a broken leg.

Of course, it probably came naturally for him, as it did for many men. Not that Brooke had seen all that many men who looked like Jared Granger. Not even close.

He seemed unaffected by Brooke's perusal, and she prayed her mouth was shut. "Where's the washer?" she asked, when what she really wanted to know was where her good sense had fled.

He pointed to a louvered door to his right. "In there."

"Okay, then. Let's see if I can figure this out." Securing the pile of towels under her chin, she opened the door and stuffed the load into the washer. After tossing a scoop of detergent in, she stared at the knobs for a few minutes.

"Mind if I throw a few more things in with those?"

The hair on Brooke's neck came to attention when she realized he was standing immediately behind her. She sensed his heat, smelled his cologne and finally got up the nerve to look at him over her shoulder. "What do you have in mind?"

He pointed to a laundry basket sitting atop the dryer. "My underwear and a few pair of socks."

She surveyed the pile of briefs in the basket. Not

surprising. He seemed like a brief kind of guy. "I have room for a few. Nothing worse than being down to your last pair."

"I ran out two days ago."

That thought conjured up all sorts of questions she didn't dare ask. She didn't have to.

"I'm going native," he said. "That's what we used to call it in college when we ran out of Jockey shorts. In case you're wondering."

She *had* been wondering, and going "native" seemed an appropriate description. Right now she was having some fairly primitive thoughts about the man behind her. "Do you want me to teach you how to use the washer?" Her voice came out highpitched and shaky.

"Nope. I can handle the washer. I manage fine with my left hand."

Then why hadn't he? Maybe he was playing on her sympathy, knowing she'd feel sorry for him and engage in some menial tasks. Then again, maybe he truly didn't have the energy.

After tossing a few pair of underwear into the washer with the towels, Brooke turned to find Jared Granger seated at the table. He'd actually retrieved a basin and filled it with water while she'd been taking care of the laundry. So he wasn't helpless after all. But he was gorgeous sitting there with his bare chiseled chest and tousled blond hair. A woman could sure get a thrill running her hands over all that sinewy muscle.

Brooke slapped the thoughts out of her brain. For goodness' sake, it wasn't like she hadn't seen a half-naked man before. Just not any who had the kind of sensual aura that made women take a second look. A third look…

What was it about him that made her feel all soggy inside? Why did she respond to his questionable comments when she had learned long ago not to react to anything with sexual undercurrents where patients were concerned? Where any man was concerned, for that matter.

Right now she didn't care to dissect her reaction to Jared Granger. Right now she only had to help the man shave. And Lord help her, she hoped she survived it.

Three

The woman had great hands, and she had them on him.

With a cheerful smile, Brooke lathered Jared's jaw with shaving cream, patting his cheeks like a kid having a fine time playing in the mud. But the way his body was reacting, she might as well have her great hands farther south.

Nope, he wasn't dead. At least not all of him. Jared realized that the moment she'd started cutting away his beard. There was something innately intimate about a woman doing this to him. About Brooke Lewis doing this to him, he corrected. Who would've thought that something as elemental as getting a shave would be such a turn-on?

He shifted in his seat on that thought.

"Hold still," she said. "I don't want this all over me."

Jared met Brooke's gaze to find she was concentrating on getting the shaving cream in all the right places. Hell, at this rate, she'd be here until dawn. And he'd be a raving lunatic because, at the moment, her breasts were about level with his mouth. If he moved just a hair forward, he could plant his foamed-up face right into her knit-covered cleavage.

"Do you want to try it?"

Oh, yeah, he did. Thankfully she moved away before he could give everything over to impulse.

"I think you've done enough playing with the lotion," he said. And it was playing on his nerve endings in a not too bad way, as well as other places.

She put the can of cream down on the table beside her and picked up the razor. "I meant do you want to try using this."

"I already have. I nicked myself about fifty times the last time I gave it the old collegiate try."

"Okay. Let's see if we can figure this out." After placing the razor back on the table, she removed the towel she'd draped over his chest, shook out the hair clippings onto a newspaper she'd placed on the floor, then bent forward again to reknot it at his neck. All the while, Jared considered what it would be like to grab her around the waist, pull her between his parted legs and plant a kiss on that sassy mouth of hers.

He damned his near loss of control. What was it about Brooke Lewis that had his imagination running helter-skelter? Because she'd treated him as though she understood his dilemma? Because she was a woman and readily available? He only wished that were the case. It was more complicated than that. She was more complicated than that.

"Okay, let's get started." Moving behind him, she grabbed up the razor and handed it over his shoulder. "Let's see what you can do with this."

He curled the offending object, his recent nemesis, in his left fingers and stared into the mirror she'd set up on the table. He managed to shave his left cheek okay, and his jaw with only a slight nick. But when it came to his upper lip, no go. If he tried to use his right hand to manipulate his nose, his stiff fingers got in the way.

When he did give it a shot, the razor dropped onto his lap. They both reached for it at the same time.

"I've got it," he said, rougher than he'd intended. But her hand was just inches away from dangerous territory. And one bad thing about going native—tough to hide your sins. His fingers weren't the only thing that was stiff.

She cleared her throat. "I see what you mean about this being hard."

That was the understatement of the millennium. "Yeah, it's hard, all right."

She moved to his side, a soft blush staining her fair cheeks. "So I'll just help you this time, and hopefully you'll get some more use out of those fingers in the near future. Then you can go back to doing it yourself."

That wasn't at all what he had in mind. "Ah, now, that's no fun. Why would I want to do it myself when you could do a much better job?"

Her dark eyes narrowed. "Do I look like a slave to you?"

No, but she sure looked great with her hair curling around her face and her full lips trying hard not to smile. "Seems to me, Ms. Lewis, that since I'm in the chair with a cracked leg and a sorry hand, and you're holding the razor, that pretty much makes me a slave to your whims."

"Put your knees together," she said.

Man, she *had* noticed. "Why?"

"So I can get to you better"

She was already getting to him. *Really* getting to him. After he complied, she stood in front of him again, this time straddling his legs stretched out before him, thankfully avoiding his cast. If she tripped, she'd end up on top of him, and God only knew what he would do then. Nothing that would be appropriate.

She tilted his head back to shave his neck up to his chin. "And what whims do you think I might be entertaining, Dr. Granger?"

"Cutting my throat?" He'd be cutting his own throat if he didn't watch what he said from here on out. She might just turn tail and run.

This time she smiled as she swished the razor in the basin then brought it back to his chin. "I doubt I could do that with this thing, but you've just given me an idea. I planned to bring an electric razor when I came back. Instead, I'll bring a straight razor. How's that?"

"No need to use force. Just tell me what you need, and I'll do my damnedest to comply." And whatever she needed, he'd willingly give it to her, even if it took all night.

Her blush deepened as if she'd read his mind. It made her all the more pretty. All the more tempting. "Right now just be still. We're almost done here, then I need to go."

Jared didn't want to be still. He couldn't be still. Not with her so close that he could experience her heat, smell her clean woman's scent mixed with the smell of his shaving cream. Not when she had her long fingers framing his face while the steady brush of the razor over his beard kept time with his pounding pulse. Not when he had a bird's-eye view of her white knit shirt pulled tight, revealing the outline of her bra and high round breasts.

"Okay, all done." She stepped away from him and dropped the razor into the basin, then stood studying her handiwork. "Wow, you almost look civilized."

Jared didn't feel the least bit civilized. In fact, he felt untamed, wild with some deep-seated need to pull her into his lap, take the can of shaving cream and make good use of it in other, more interesting endeavors. Take that hellacious lab coat off her shoulders and see exactly what was underneath.

"Great," he said to keep from groaning. "I'm glad I got through that relatively unscathed." Relatively was the key word in this instance.

She braced one hand on her hip and tossed her curls away from her face with the other hand. "Admit it, Dr. Granger. I did a great job."

He ran a hand over his jaw. "Yeah, you did a great job."

"Thanks." She grinned.

And Jared's heart nearly came to a complete stop. Suddenly he didn't want her to leave. He wanted her to stay, if only to enjoy her company and nothing more. But he wouldn't ask that of her. Not tonight.

She picked up her bag while he struggled to get up from the chair. His butt was numb from sitting so long. Not that he'd run any races lately. But he had walked around the acreage some, when he wasn't stretched out on the sofa watching sports on TV.

He followed her out the door and once on the porch, she turned to him. "I expect that when I return on Monday, I'll find you've been doing your home therapy more often."

He braced his crutch under his arm and gave her a less-than-enthusiastic left-handed salute. "You bet, captain."

"And when I come back, I'm hoping that maybe you'll have called your housekeeper to come clean some of the mess."

"I'll think about it. If you'll do me another favor."

She leaned one shoulder against the wall and sighed. "What is it this time? Clean your oven?"

He couldn't contain his smile. "Nothing like that. Next time you come here, wear your street clothes. You're in the country, and this is my home, not the hospital."

She studied him a long moment. "Yeah, you're absolutely right. This isn't the hospital. I'll be sure to wear jeans. How's that?"

"Suits me fine." He could just imagine Brooke in jeans, and that thought almost unraveled his slender thread of control.

She checked her watch. "It's late. I better get going."

He hadn't even noticed the time. She'd made the hours pass quickly with her easy conversation and acerbic wit. And he still didn't want her to go.

"You know, I should've had you come earlier so you wouldn't be driving home in the dark," he said to buy a few more minutes. "Why don't you come at five next time?

"Okay. I'll rearrange my schedule."

He rested against the wall, facing her. "Do you want me to ride back into town with you?"

"Then how would you get back?"

"I wouldn't have to come back. I could spend the night on your sofa." Now why the hell had he said that?

She gave him a disparaging look. "Yeah, right. My sister is between apartments right now. She's on my sofa."

"Is she as pretty as you?"

Her blush made another appearance. "Actually, much prettier."

"I seriously doubt that."

"Don't. It's true."

He didn't believe it for a minute. Not with those dark eyes and darker curls that made her look wild and wanton, as if she'd just left a lover's arms. Not with that innocent face and upturned nose, her naturally rosy cheeks...with residual shaving cream smeared upward toward her eye.

Crooking a finger at her, he said, "Come here."

She looked almost alarmed, as if he'd asked her to strip. "Why?"

"You have some shaving cream on your face. It's easier for you to move."

She inched a little closer. He cupped her cheek with his good hand and swiped the splotch away with his thumb. The moment suspended while Jared battled what he should do, and what he really wanted to do— kiss her. Test the textures of her sweet, sensual mouth and lose all his worries in her. But good sense won the war, and he dropped his hand.

She turned her eyes to the weathered wood column holding up the porch. "Look, Dr. Granger—"

"You can call me Jared."

She caught his gaze again. "No, I really can't. In order to maintain our professional arrangement, we need to keep this on a professional level."

"And that's not what we've been doing?"

"Well, yes. And no."

He braced his left hand against the wall above her head. "Tell me about the no part."

She lifted one shoulder in a shrug. "I've really enjoyed getting to know you better, but—well, at times..." She threaded her bottom lip between her teeth and her gaze faltered.

Jared leaned a little closer. "At times you felt something stirring between us tonight?"

"Maybe. I don't know."

"Brooke, look at me." She did, slowly. "I'm not going to do anything to jeopardize your job, if that's what you're worried about. Especially since I know firsthand what it's like to lose a career."

He took in a deep draw of air and released it on a sigh. "And, yeah, maybe I got a little out of hand tonight. But you're a very attractive woman, and it's been a long time since I've enjoyed being around anyone. But if we're going to spend time together, I'd rather us be friends than enemies. That's all it is."

That wasn't it at all. He knew it, and she probably knew it. They'd just have to deal with it when the time came. And the time would come. Sooner than she realized, if he had any say in the matter.

"Okay, then," she said with a hesitant smile. "I can do the friend thing, as long as you remember who's the boss."

He gave her a responding grin. "Hell, I knew that the day I met you. But you'll have to be patient with me. I'm usually in charge."

She winked, sending his pulse on another marathon. "Yeah, I know, and it's a real power trip, isn't it?"

He laughed then, an honest-to-goodness laugh that made him feel more energetic than he had in weeks. "Are you sure you don't want me to ride home with you? I can take a cab back in. No problem, really."

She slipped her slender fingers in the bag and pulled out her cell phone. "I have this, and my can of pepper mace, and a baseball bat in the back seat of my car. If I can't bring 'em down with the mace, I can hit a moving target without any problem using the bat."

Jared let go a loud wince. "First the razor, then the bat. Remind me not to really tick you off."

"Don't worry, I will." With that, she hurried down the steps and slid into her car.

"Be careful," Jared called out to her.

She stuck her hand out the window and gave him the okay sign.

Even after the taillights disappeared from view, he still stood there watching the empty space where her car had been, fighting the loneliness that was so much a part of his life of late. Fighting the strong attraction for Brooke Lewis—his therapist—a struggle he wasn't sure he could win.

More important, he wasn't sure he wanted to.

* * *

She couldn't do it anymore. Not after last night. Not after that near-miss kiss. Not after battling an attraction that defied all logic.

She had to resign as his therapist as much as she hated the prospect. As much as she hated that she hated it.

Brooke shoved one last bite of wilted Waldorf salad into her mouth, oblivious to the sounds surrounding her in the hospital cafeteria, the steady drone of conversation and the rattle of utensils, until she heard Dr. Kempner's voice coming from behind her.

She sneaked a glance over her shoulder and saw him sitting with a colleague who took that opportune moment to get up and walk away. Now he was alone, and she had her chance to do what she had to do.

After dabbing at her mouth with a napkin, Brooke stood and slid her tray from the table then walked to the nearby conveyor belt to discard it. Once she was finished disposing of what was left of her less-than-memorable lunch, she held her breath and turned back to see if Dr. Kempner was still seated. Luckily, he was, and no one had joined him. Amazing, considering he was as in demand as Jared Granger among the single crowd. He drew more attention than a code blue in ICU.

Brooke had to admit, he was more than attractive, but where Nick Kempner was known for his bad-boy charm, Jared Granger had that mysterious quality, the guarded persona that kept you guessing. Kept you wondering what he was thinking. What he was feeling. For Brooke, that element and so many others held a lot of appeal....

She slapped her thoughts back in order. Why couldn't she get the man off her mind? She likened Jared Granger to a bad case of Asian flu—fever inducing, shake provoking and definitely hard to get out of the system. Not much choice but to let him run his course with plenty of bed rest. Thinking about settling into bed with Jared Granger didn't help Brooke's mental state in the least. Hopefully she could carry on a decent conversation with Dr. Kempner.

Slowly she strolled toward the table and once there, cleared the desert-like dryness from her throat. "Dr. Kempner, do you have a minute?"

He looked up with a guarded expression, probably expecting some fawning nurse with a major case of the hots for him. Once he recognized her, he smiled. "Sure thing, Brooke. I've been meaning to talk to you about Dr. Granger's therapy."

She couldn't have wished for a better opening, yet she was instantly filled with dread. What if Jared Granger had already decided to let her out of the arrangement? That would certainly make things easier, since that's exactly what she intended to do, remove herself as his therapist. Then why did she suddenly feel so terribly disappointed?

Dr. Kempner stood, rounded the table and pulled her chair back. "Have a seat."

Brooke complied and clasped her hands in her lap while he took the chair across from her. She didn't want her serious case of nerves exposed by her trembling fingers. "Actually," she began, "I wanted to talk about Dr. Granger, too."

"Good, because I just got off the phone with him. I don't know what you've been doing, but I hope you keep doing it."

She felt as though someone had clamped her lungs with a hemostat. "Come again?"

Kempner leaned back in his seat and ran a hand through his dark hair. "I haven't heard him sound this upbeat since the accident. He's enthusiastic about continuing. Very enthusiastic. It's the first time he's said he thinks he might be able to return to surgery."

"He really said that?"

Dr. Kempner's grin expanded. "Yeah. That's what he said. You're the best thing that's happened to him in a long time. And suggesting the home therapy has made him do a complete turnaround. Wish I'd thought of it. He might have been farther along in his recovery if I had. As far as I'm concerned, you've just worked a miracle."

Brooke had been complimented on her techniques before, but usually by patients, not attending physicians. She couldn't contain the little nip of pride. "Well, I'm glad to hear he's more positive. But I'm not sure my continuing his therapy is such a good idea."

Kempner leaned forward and toyed with a spoon. "I don't understand. Seems to me Jared's very happy with you."

"I'm glad." More glad than he realized, and that was the problem. "I'm just wondering if someone else might do a better job. Maybe someone with more experience. Maybe even an OT."

He stopped spinning the spoon and gave her a

questioning look. "You've been at this for how long?"

"Five years, including clinicals."

"I'd say that qualifies you as experienced."

Yes, but she wasn't equipped to handle Jared Granger and all his sexuality. "I suppose so."

"Are you sure there's not another problem?"

Oh, heavens, was her face a billboard? "What do you mean?"

"I mean is he still giving you trouble."

The good Dr. Granger had been giving her trouble, all right. The kind of trouble that came calling when a woman noticed a man on a very elemental level. The kind of trouble that kept her up nights, all night, with thoughts of him darting in and out of her head until she could do nothing more than toss and turn like a practiced insomniac. Brooke didn't dare admit that to this doctor, though. "So far he's been reluctant to do his home program." At least that sounded logical.

"Oh, he's doing it, all right. Three times today already."

Brooke couldn't stop her satisfied smile. "Really?"

"Yeah. And he asked if he could increase your sessions to three times a week instead of two. I'd say that's incentive enough for you to continue as planned."

Other incentives concerned Brooke more, like Jared's blue eyes, his large hands, his athlete's physique... Now when did she start thinking of him as just "Jared"?

She pinched the bridge of her nose and closed her eyes. This would never do.

The annoying shrill of a beeper brought her attention back to Dr. Kempner, who was busy checking his pager. He quickly stood and said, "Gotta run. It's surgery. They've probably moved up my next case up."

"Hey, Brookie," came from across the room, stopping Nick Kempner's departure.

This was all she needed, Michelle yelling her silly nickname across a crowded hospital cafeteria.

Dr. Kempner looked toward a smiling Michelle, then back at Brooke. "Do you know her?"

Was it a sin to deny your kin? "At the moment I'd like to say no—but, yeah, I know her. Very well. She's my sister."

Dr. Kempner looked more than mildly interested in Michelle as she tossed her mane of dark hair over her shoulder, unmindful of the attention she was drawing from the surgeon, and probably every other doc in the place. Nothing new there.

"Does she work here?" he asked.

"Yeah. She's the new PR person."

He still didn't take his eyes off Michelle, as if she were some kind of man magnet. Nothing new there, either. "I've never seen her before," he said.

Well, now you have, and a picture would last longer, Brooke wanted to say. Instead, she settled for, "About Dr. Granger. I really think—"

"Oh, yeah. Dr. Granger." He finally dragged his gaze away from Michelle and picked up his tray. "I'll change the order to three times a week. You two can work out the schedule. Keep up the good work."

With that he was gone in a rush, nothing more than a streak of blue scrubs and cocky confidence.

What just happened? Obviously, she'd been rail-roaded. Now she had no choice but to continue Jared Granger's therapy, at least for the time being. At least until he got a little better. Which meant more visits to his home, more hand holding, more up-close-and-personal contact with a testosterone-laden male trying to prove he still had what it took to seduce a woman. And, boy, did he.

She would simply have to stay strong. Ignore those things that touched her on a very feminine level, right to the carnal core of her. And that would be about as easy as disregarding a nuclear bomb in her own back-yard. Something would have to give, and it certainly wasn't going to be her.

Four

Jared normally wasn't a clock watcher, but as the time approached 5 p.m., he started counting minutes. Pretty damned ridiculous that he would get so excited about his visiting therapist. But it wasn't the therapy he looked forward to. The thought of seeing Brooke again had his motor running at full speed.

For the past two weeks she had been in his home on a regular basis, always maintaining a professional demeanor while administering therapy. Yet more and more Jared had come to appreciate the little things about Brooke Lewis—her easy conversation, gentle touch and bright smile. All served to ease the weight of his predicament. She had an uncanny knack of keeping him grounded while prodding him to work harder in his recovery. He certainly didn't resent her tenacity; he had come to welcome it. And with each visit, he had fought a very primal need to get to know her on a level that went far beyond the patient-therapist relationship. But he'd kept those urges in check. He feared that if he didn't, she might never come back. Yet he wasn't sure how long he could fight the inadvisable attraction.

Jared gave himself a mental pep talk. He needed to keep everything in perspective. Keep his hands to himself except during treatments. Keep everything in control, including his persistent libido.

If he moved at the rate his hormones demanded, she'd be out of his life in a flash, taking her skill and those healing hands with her.

But when the knock came at the door, he managed to answer the summons in record time. At least now he was getting around better, thanks to his new cast. But he still wasn't capable of running any marathons or chasing after a reluctant woman.

That thought brought about a smile as he opened the door.

Brooke stood on the porch, her back to him, watching the sunset, he guessed. The copper-orange sky set off the burnished highlights in her hair, something he hadn't noticed before. He had noticed other things about her since she'd started dressing in casual clothing for the sessions. Today she wore a pair of faded jeans and a loose flannel shirt, the tail covering most of her bottom. When she turned, he noted the shirt gaped open, revealing another white knit top much like the one she'd worn underneath the awful lab coat. A top that hugged her breasts like a second skin.

"Hi. Nice evening we're having," she said.

"Yeah. Kind of warm." Or was it her presence that made the cool fall evening unseasonably arid?

He hobbled onto the porch and stood before her, resisting the urge to reach out and run his functioning hand through that wild tangle of silky curls.

"Where's your crutch?" she asked.

"Don't need it."

She glanced at his broken leg. "A walking cast, I see. That's got to be a whole lot better."

"Much better." He held up his hand. "And so is this." Concentrating on his injured fingers, he bent them forward. Not even close to a fist, but much better, except for the second digit that didn't seem to be healing like the rest.

She applauded and gave him the luminous smile he was growing far too fond of. "Bravo, Dr. Granger. I see you've been a good boy."

Right now he felt like a bad boy. He had the strongest urge to pull her into his arms for a long embrace, both out of gratitude and the overwhelming need to touch her. Calling up his control, he dropped his hand to his side and slipped the other in his pocket. "I've been working hard, like you asked. And I think this calls for a celebration of sorts."

Her smile faded into a frown. "What do you have in mind?"

"How about taking a walk before it gets dark?"

"What about your treatment?"

"We can do that when we get back. It can't be too long a walk considering my limitations." He tapped the heel of his cast on the wooden floor. "Unless you have other plans for the evening." If not, he'd walk a mile to be in her company.

"No. No plans. But I think it might be better if we—"

"Come on, Brooke. A short walk down the path." He pointed toward a small clump of oaks a few yards away. "Just to right over there."

She glanced over her shoulder at the place he'd indicated. "Okay. I can manage that. It would probably do me good to get some exercise."

He sent her a satisfied smile. "It'll do us both good."

While Jared slowly hobbled down the three steps, Brooke waited patiently at the bottom. She didn't take his hand to assist him, something Jared appreciated on one level. On another, he wished she would. He had some irrepressible need to have her hands on him. But she would soon enough, at least during therapy. He would have to settle for the limited contact, no matter how much he craved more.

She moved easily back into the professional mode, keeping her distance as they walked through the metal gate and onto the path leading to the area scaling the southwest corner of the pasture. A long span of silence stretched between them, disturbed only by the occasional call of a bird and the rustle of dried grass beneath their feet.

Jared nodded toward a place alongside the path a few feet ahead. "That's where it happened."

Brooke stared at the tractor sitting like a monument to his carelessness. "It hasn't been moved?"

"Nope. I couldn't do it, and I really don't have anyone who can do it for me."

"No friends?"

"Maybe Kempner, but he's not too keen on farm

implements. He's only interested in the kind of equipment that comes with the feminine persuasion.''

Brooke laughed softly. ''Surely he's not that bad.''

Jared smiled. ''Not as bad as most people think. He's pretty much sworn off women since his divorce, or so he says.''

''How about you?''

He'd had his share of women, but until recently, he hadn't found one that could hold his interest for very long. Not until he'd met Brooke. He glanced at her and could tell she'd regretted the question by the self-conscious look on her face.

''Nick's divorce hasn't affected me one way or the other,'' he said, trying to lighten the mood.

''What about that Candy woman?''

There was a name he didn't care to hear. A woman he didn't care to remember. ''How did you know about her?''

''Nothing's sacred at Memorial. And I saw you with her on TV one time, when she was reporting on the hospital fund-raiser for the new pediatric unit.''

Jared paused for the flock of birds taking flight in a flurry of beating wings. He wanted to make sure she heard what he had to say about Candy Rawlings. Make sure she had no doubt that he wasn't interested in a woman whose major goal was to snare a wealthy doctor. ''The best thing I can say about Candy is that she's very confident. Unfortunately, I didn't like her as much as she liked her.''

''Interesting.'' Brooke smiled, flashing him a dimple and a cynical look. ''So she wasn't exactly a love interest.''

''Do you mean were we lovers?''

Her eyes widened, and she looked away. "No, that's not what I meant—I mean—I meant..." She crossed her arms over her middle. "I'm sorry. That was an intrusive question. It's really none of my business."

He stopped in the path. "Since you asked, yes, we were involved for a while. At the moment there's no one special, if that's what you really wanted to know."

She faced him, arms still tightly crossed. "Tell me about the accident. How did it happen?"

Her change of subject was as smooth as satin. Just one more of her talents. If he had his way, he'd discover them all. If he didn't stop thinking of her on those terms, he'd try to find out about those talents right here, right now, in the middle of nature and let nature take its course.

Jared swiped up a stalk of grass then tossed it away, wishing he could as easily discard the memories. "The accident was a result of sheer stupidity. I wasn't paying attention. A wire got caught in the shredder. I tried to yank it out without turning off the tractor. It slashed across my wrist, then I landed wrong on my left side with my leg underneath me. Broke my tibia pretty well. Luckily I had my cell phone and a bandanna to wrap my wrist, otherwise I might've bled to death waiting for the damned paramedics. Took them twenty minutes to get here."

"That must have been torture."

"Yeah. Not one of my finer moments, that's for sure."

But he was having one now. When she started up the path again, Jared followed a few steps behind sim-

ply to enjoy the way soft flannel and washed-out
denim shaped her fine-looking bottom, revealing hips
that were naturally round. He'd had his fill of model-
types with more bones than flesh. He liked a little
extra padding that he could get his hands on and feel
as though he really had hold of something worthwhile. Something real. Brooke was real and whole-
some. A natural woman. All woman.

"I guess you come out here to get away from it
all," she said, disrupting his pleasant assessment.

He turned his thoughts to the past few weeks and
the farm. The place had proven to be a great escape.
In some ways the consummate prison. "Yeah. That's
what I was doing that weekend, getting away. I lost
a patient the day before. A young girl. It pretty much
tore me up. I had my mind on that, not my business."

He couldn't imagine why he was spilling his guts
to Brooke Lewis, but for some reason he thought she
might understand. He'd never told anyone how much
Kayla Brown's death had affected him. How helpless
he'd felt. Losing some of that burden lightened the
weight on his heart.

She halted and turned to him. "I'm sorry. I didn't
know. That must be so tough, losing a patient. I don't
know how you do it, day in, day out."

"The same way you do."

"But my patients are there after the fact, to get
better. I don't know how I'd handle losing one."

Without thought he took two steps forward, close
enough to reach up and brush a stray curl from her
brow. "You would. If you can handle me, you can
handle anything."

She narrowed her eyes like a gunslinger about to

deliver a dead-on shot. "You're not so tough, Dr. Granger."

He sighed. "Would you call me Jared?"

Her gaze slid away. "You know I can't do that."

"Then call me 'pain in the butt,' 'idiot,' anything but 'doctor.' I might have to give that title up, so I'd better get used to it."

She propped one hand on her hip and glared at him. "I refuse to let you talk that way. I refuse to hear any more nonsense about giving up your goals to return to surgery, and even if you can't operate again, God forbid, you're still a doctor, and you always will be. Is that understood?"

Jared grinned at the flash of fire in her dark eyes, the firm set of her great mouth. "You know, you're really beautiful when you're mad."

"Then I must be Miss Universe at the moment because if you keep talking that way, then I'll just have to—"

He cut off her tirade with a kiss. He couldn't help it. All that passion had fueled his own, and he couldn't fight it anymore. He didn't expect that she would respond, but her lips parted, either at his insistence or her shock, and he took immediate advantage. He slipped his tongue inside the pleasant heat of her mouth, slow and restrained, although it was all he could do not to deepen the kiss, make it hotter than a three-alarm blaze.

Surprisingly, she didn't push him away. Instead she began to actively participate in the exploration, touching her tongue tentatively to his, giving him one hell of a jolt. He wrapped his splinted hand around her waist and hooked his left thumb in the belt loop above her back pocket. If he were more mobile, he'd pull her closer or lay her down.

That thought shot a spear of heat straight to his groin. If he didn't stop, he might embarrass himself. Embarrass them both. It had been way too long since he'd wanted a woman this much. He couldn't even remember when he *had* wanted a woman this badly. All the more reason to stop.

Then she draped her arms around his neck and slid her fingers through the hair above his nape. Ending the impulsive act wasn't an option, now that she was completely against him, molded to him, making him feel alive. Filling him with a hunger he could barely contain. He hoped she was so lost in this kiss that she didn't notice what was going on below his belt. Hard to ignore something so obvious.

Suddenly Brooke pushed against his chest and stepped back. More than likely he'd been caught.

She grabbed her hair as if she wanted to pull it out by the roots. "What is wrong with me?"

"Not a damned thing."

"Oh, yeah, there is. I've totally lost my mind."

"You look okay to me." And beautiful with her swollen lips and flushed cheeks.

"Well, I'm not okay. I'm crazy."

So was he, about her. He'd have to analyze that later, when he was alone and could think straight.

She began to stride up the path toward the house, leaving Jared struggling to keep up with her. "Slow down or I'm going to land flat on my face," he said.

She measured her steps somewhat, but not as much as Jared would have liked. He managed to catch her arm, bringing her to a halt. Her eyes were all fire and frustration. He wanted to kiss her again. Not a good idea at the moment.

"I'm sorry," he said, although he wasn't. "I couldn't help myself."

"Well I should've been able to help myself. We both know we can't do this."

"We already did, and damned well if I do say so myself."

"Yeah, boy." Her tone was pure sarcasm.

"Are you telling me you didn't enjoy it?" His laugh was abrupt. "You could've fooled me."

She rolled her eyes. "No, that's not what I'm telling you. I did enjoy it, and that's the problem. So are you satisfied, *Doctor?*"

No, he wasn't. He wouldn't be satisfied until he could witness all that passion in bed. Not until he could experience all that fire when he made love to her, and that's exactly what he intended to do, and soon. He'd just have to take it slow, at least wait until he got the blasted cast off his leg. Not to mention that Brooke Lewis wasn't ready to jump into his arms, much less jump his bones, at least not now. But she would be. He knew what women liked; he'd discovered that early on. He hadn't suffered through all those anatomy classes for the sole purpose of learning how to treat patients. If she would give him the chance, he'd put that knowledge to good use.

At the moment she looked as though she could cold-cock him. Time to turn on the charm, if he remembered how. A long time had passed since he'd wanted to charm anyone.

He started with a smile. "Brooke, take it easy. It was just a kiss." A mind-blowing kiss that still had him quaking inside. "This doesn't change anything between us." Thank God it wasn't storming. He'd be struck down for telling one gargantuan lie.

She gave him the most derisive look he'd ever seen. "You are so wrong. But I don't want to talk about it. Let's go back to the house and do your therapy, the reason why I'm here."

"Okay." No use arguing with her now, even though what he really wanted was another kind of therapy. The kind that would leave them both panting from exertion and wanting more.

Once they made it inside the house, Brooke went about the business of playing therapist. She set out her equipment without looking at him. She administered the treatment without speaking, except to comment on how nice the place looked, thanks to his housekeeper, who'd managed to come and clean up the day before.

He hated Brooke's silence and began to hate his lack of judgment. He knew better than to push her, and he had done exactly that when he'd kissed her. Not that he regretted it for a minute. He just hoped she would come back again. He couldn't stand the thought of her leaving him for good. That made him take another mental step back.

Midway through the therapy, her already-fair skin began to pale even more. Jared watched her struggle with her breathing and was immediately concerned.

"Are you okay?" he asked.

She reached into her canvas bag and withdrew two inhalers, took a deep draw on both, then leaned back in the chair. After a moment she croaked out the word, "Allergies."

"Asthma."

"Never try to fool a doctor," she said wryly, then shoved her inhalers back in the bag.

Jared cursed the fact that his spontaneous kiss might have upset her enough to bring on an attack. "Why didn't you tell me sooner?"

She shrugged. "It's no big deal. I've learned to live with it." She took in a ragged breath and released it slowly. At least she sounded more normal. "Sometimes it tries to get the best of me, but I refuse to let it bring me down."

Jared's respect for her increased tenfold. Here she was, living with an ongoing disease and staying in the groove of life without a second thought. She inspired him to get better. To try harder. Not only for himself, but also for her.

"Adult onset, or have you always had it?" he asked, truly wanting to know this—and more—about her.

A flash of pain crossed her expression. "For as long as I can remember. Just one of those things that hangs around like an annoying relative. You learn to ignore it, but every now and then it comes back to remind you it's still there."

"If you had told me then I wouldn't have—"

"Kissed me?" She emphasized the question by raising a thin dark brow. "I'm not going to go belly-up after a kiss."

"I'm not saying that. I'm saying I would've warned you first."

She went back to massaging his hand. "No offense, Doctor, but it was probably just the high mold count, not the kiss."

"Man, you sure know how to shred a guy's ego."

Her grin came out of hiding. "I try."

He placed his left hand on her right one so she'd stop the massage. "Are you saying that kiss didn't leave you even a little breathless?"

She pinned him with those dark eyes, but this time he didn't see anger or regret. More like resignation. "Okay, maybe a teeny-weeny little bit."

"I'm glad, because on a scale of one to ten, I'd say it was about a twenty."

She tilted her head and frowned. "Would you stop doing that?"

He moved his hand away. "Sorry. I forget you have a job to do."

"Not that. I meant would you stop flirting with me."

"Is that what I'm doing?"

"You know darn well it is." More skepticism in her expression and tone.

"Can't help myself."

"I think I liked you better the other way."

"What way was that?"

"When you were mad at me."

He tipped her chin, forcing her to look at him. "I wasn't mad at you. I was mad at me. At the world. At the injustice of this damned injury. I'm not anymore, or at least not all the time. I have you to thank for that."

"Don't thank me. You've done it on your own."

"No, I haven't. You're partially responsible. If it hadn't been for you, I probably would've given up."

She looked away again. "Anyone could have done it."

"You're wrong, Brooke. Dead wrong."

* * *

She might be wrong about her contribution to his therapy, Brooke thought, but she wasn't wrong about her instincts. What had happened between them—was happening—wasn't appropriate.

They why did it feel so right?

That didn't matter. What she knew to be the truth did. Involvement with a patient was forbidden. Her head knew that all too well, even if her heart refused to heed the warning.

So while she faced Jared Granger in the glow of the porch light, the cool November breeze whispering across her heated skin, she prepared to tell him exactly what she knew she must before leaving for home. Maybe even leaving for good.

"Dr. Granger," she said in her most practiced voice. "I believe you're starting to experience transference. You're grateful for what I've done with your hand. It's really very common between physical therapists and patients during the course of—"

"Cut the crap, Brooke."

"What?"

"Stop treating me like a patient." His ice blue gaze began to punch holes in her resolve.

"You *are* my patient."

He took a significant step toward Brooke, almost scaling that intangible wall she'd built to protect herself from his type of magnetism. She'd been there, done that, wasn't making the trip again. She couldn't pay the price, both with the possible loss of her job and her heart.

"I wasn't your patient tonight," he said. "At least not when you were in my arms."

He didn't have to move closer to affect her. The hard set of his well-defined jaw, the intensity in his to-die-for blue eyes, his adamant yet sensual tone, threatened to destroy all her good reason. She couldn't let him do that.

"But we—"

"It's my turn to talk and your turn to listen."

Brooke opened her mouth for a moment before letting it drop shut. She'd give him his say then take her turn shooting down every one of his rationalizations when her time came. She knew firsthand how men operated. If you gave them what they needed, they eventually discarded you like fallen tree limbs after a wild summer storm. She refused to let that happen again.

If only he'd stop looking at her like that. Like a man on a mission who wouldn't stop until he got what he wanted. If only she knew for certain exactly what he did want. Admittedly, she had her suspicions. She sure didn't care for them much, even though it excited her to think he might simply want her. And that annoyed the heck out of her.

He looked almost grim, much the same as in the beginning, when he'd acted as though he couldn't stand the sight of her. "First of all, stop patronizing me, Brooke. I know what transference is. I know what it means to have a patient believe themselves in love or lust or whatever with you. It's happened to me before. Several times. With women of all ages, shapes and sizes. You save their life, you become a god. But I'm not a god. I'm only a man."

He slipped his left arm around her waist. "A man with normal needs, who appreciates a beautiful, sensual woman, even if that woman doesn't realize her appeal or her power."

With one fluid move he pulled her against his solid body. She was amazed at his strength, even more amazed at her reaction to his charismatic voice, his sensual words, the heady scent of his cologne. The feel of his solid chest pressed against her breasts and his taut thighs grazing hers staggered her senses and launched her pulse into an irregular tempo.

He rested his whisker-rough jaw against her cheek, as if to lead her in a slow dance into paradise. His lips were at her ear. His warm breath feathered her neck. "I damn well know the difference between gratitude and desire, so stop handing me that excuse. Because, babe, it's not gratitude causing this." He dropped his hand to her hip and nudged her forward. She felt his erection below her belly, and her control beginning to slip.

Desire for her? How could that be? Why her? And what had happened to her intentions of setting him straight?

She knew exactly what had happened. His sensuality had stolen the sum and substance of every argument in Brooke's professional repertoire. Her rebuttal had been replaced by a need so great she shook with the power of it. Now she bordered on taking a plunge into perilous waters with only Jared Granger to save her.

He wouldn't, though. That much she realized. He'd simply dive right in with her if given the opportunity. And deep down she knew that she was about to fall.

Five

She had primed herself for the impact of his kiss, even welcomed it. But she wasn't prepared for his sudden step back.

"Go home, Brooke," he said, his voice husky and strained. "Go home while you still can. I'll see you Monday."

With that he turned away and started toward the door.

Brooke sensed her blood pressure rising to a hazardous level. She spoke around the ringing into her ears. "Don't you dare go in that house."

He faced her again and raked a hand through his golden hair. "If I don't go in now, I'm liable to carry you in with me."

"Like some caveman? Are you going to throw me

over your shoulder? Or maybe just grab me by the hair and drag me in. I'd like to see you try."

His blues eyes flamed with challenge. "Would you?"

Uh-oh. "No. I'm not going in with you, but I'm not leaving, either. Not until we talk about this."

He slipped his left hand into his jeans pocket, the right one dangling at his side. "There's nothing more to say right now. You know how I feel. If you want to keep this on a professional level, I can accept that. But I don't accept you denying there's something going on between us."

Right now she was simply confused. She only knew she couldn't leave so much unsaid. "Maybe I shouldn't come back on Monday."

His expression softened. "I need you, Brooke, for whatever that's worth."

Hadn't she heard *that* before. *I need you, Brooke,* echoed in her ears, only the voice belonged to Brandon. *If you'll just help me get through these classes…it's for our future….*

But that future had never materialized. He'd been long gone before she realized he'd only needed her for one thing—an avenue to get his degree before he tossed her aside like yesterday's leftovers.

Brooke paced the porch, restless with the desire to hear Jared's version of the truth. The desire for him. "Do you need me as your therapist or your plaything?"

Anger flashed across his face, turning his features to granite. "I don't see you as a *plaything*. I see you as a desirable woman, and I admire your conviction as far as your job is concerned. Conviction got me a long way. But I've also learned that a career is a sorry substitute for a real life. No matter how hard you try, you'll never please everyone, so you have to please yourself."

Who had he tried to please? Another woman? "This doesn't have anything to do with my job."

"It has everything to do with your job."

"Not anymore."

"What are you saying?"

She had no idea. "I'm saying I need to think about this. Think about what I'm feeling."

"What are you feeling?"

She stomped her foot hard on the porch. "I don't know. You're making it hard to think." Hard to breathe. Hard to resist.

His smile came halfway, heralding impending victory. "Okay. So go home and think. You know where to find me."

"That's it?"

"You need something else from me?"

A frustrated groan slipped out. "I need you to understand how hard this is on me."

He had the gall to grin. "Hard on you?" He took a long lingering visual journey down her body, then back up again. She felt totally exposed and very overheated, yet she shivered under his continued perusal. "You better be damned glad I have a bad leg," he said. "Two more minutes and we might have initiated this porch."

Brooke's face blazed, both from embarrassment and the thrilling thought of making love with Jared

Granger on a porch. Or making love with him anywhere, for that matter.

She couldn't stop the appearance of her self-
conscious smile. "Well, thank the Lord for small fa-
vors. Nothing like splinters in your butt to add to the
mood."

His laugh rumbled deep in his chest. "Some sac-
rifices are worth it."

"Go to bed, Dr. Granger."

"Alone, Ms. Lewis?"

"Alone."

"You're killing me here."

She wanted to kiss him to death. "That's just my
style. Get used to it."

He winked. "I like your style and everything else."
Pulling open the screen, he asked, "Then I'll see you
Monday?" He sounded so hopeful she almost gave
in. Almost.

"I said I have to think about it."

He streaked a hand over his shaded jaw. "Well, I
hope you do come back. I might get this damned cast
off on Tuesday. I'd like to have a real bath before my
appointment. I'm getting pretty tired of taking sponge
baths. I could use your help."

Brooke scrubbed her hands down her arms, suddenly chilled, but definitely not from the weather. He
couldn't very well get his cast too wet, and since he
only had one hand available to him, that could be very
problematic when trying to take a bath. "Aren't you
using a shower chair?"

"In case you haven't noticed, I don't have a
shower here. Just the tub. An old tub."

"What about your house in the city?"

"Yeah, I have showers there. But I prefer to be here, away from everything."

Away from reality, Brooke thought. Avoiding reminders by staying secluded. Indulging in some self-torture. But at the expense of being able to bathe himself?

How horrible to think that someone of his caliber had to forgo a real bath. Obviously he was managing okay. She'd never failed to detect a trace of spicy cologne from the first day he had come to see her.

But still, not having a good scrub in the tub now and then wasn't at all appealing to her, and she imagined not to him, either.

Brooke bit the inside of her cheek to thwart the offer threatening to spill out. No way would she do it. No way could she help him bathe. Nope, not her....

"I guess I could try to help you with a bath." Did she really say that?

He looked as surprised as she felt. "Of course, I guess it could be a problem since you're not all that big, and I'm anything but small."

She'd just bet there wasn't one small thing about him. Considering the size of his hands, his feet, she imagined most everything on him—

What was she thinking?

Thrusting away the sudden image of Jared Granger naked in the tub, she cleared the hitch from her throat and prayed her face didn't look as fiery as it felt. "Believe me, I'm stronger than you think. I have to be, especially in this line of work. But that's not what I'm worried about."

His slow-burn smile made another appearance. "What are you really worried about, Brooke? Me? I promise to be good."

His idea of *good* was probably at odds with hers. "That's what worries me."

His smile faded. "You really don't have to be afraid of me, Brooke. I'm not going to hurt you."

The way he spoke in that mellow, husky voice, Brooke almost believed him, but deep down she knew better. He could very well hurt her, even if he didn't intend to. But not if she didn't let him.

Without speaking, she turned and headed to her car, knowing that if he invited her in one more time, she might actually agree. He was wearing her down, one sensual smile, one sexy word at a time. Before long she'd be nothing more than a dusty pile of feminine need, ready to be swept up by the oh-so-sexy Dr. Jared Granger, if she wasn't careful.

She would definitely have to think about what came next. Could she allow that much intimacy by helping him bathe? Could she afford to jeopardize her job for the sake of a fling with an enigmatic doctor with an incredible body and a come-on line as big as Texas? But more important, was the possibility of falling into Jared Granger's arms, knowing the consequences, worth the risk to her fragile heart?

Jared didn't bother going to bed. Stripping out of all his clothes, he stretched out on the couch and thought about Brooke. About what she had done to his body and what she was doing to his brain.

Maybe she was right. Maybe her reluctance didn't

have anything to do with her job. Why would she want a man who might be washed up in his career? A man who had no plans for the next day or the next except to hope that he healed? Healed and returned to his only salvation, his work.

And what did he really want from Brooke? He wasn't good at personal relationships. His father was a master at emotional avoidance; just ask his mother. They stayed together for the sake of appearances. As far as Jared knew, they never really loved each other. At least it never seemed that way.

Jared's childhood memories involved parties and social climbing, his father's absence, his mother's silence. Sure, they had told him often how proud they were that he had received his M.D. Why wouldn't they be proud? Their only child had carried on their legacy. A third-generation doctor. Like his father and grandfather before him, he'd specialized in cardiac surgery.

At times Jared wondered exactly whom he'd tried to please when he entered the medical field—himself or his father? But he couldn't consider doing anything else. The love of surgery, of healing, pulsed through his veins as steadily as his blood did. Until now medicine was all that mattered. He had never even considered settling down because he'd never learned how to make a relationship with a woman work. Most people learned by example, and his example had fallen short.

So, did he really believe that Brooke Lewis could change that about him after thirty-six years? Or was it simply lust? Gratitude?

No. It was more. Maybe more than he could handle, and that scared the hell out of him.

Dr. Jared Granger was a master at mending hearts. Repairing them. Replacing them. Striving to make them good as new. Problem was, he had no idea how to tackle his own.

Brooke rushed into the apartment, gasping for air. The door slammed behind her, shaking the walls with a vengeance.

Her lungs burned, every breath an effort in futility. Panic clawed at her tightening chest. Dizziness washed over her in strong waves. Nausea knotted her belly.

She grabbed for the first inhaler on the end table and drew deep, once, twice. She coughed several times. More burning, more wheezing. She grabbed the second inhaler, sucked in more medication, then coughed again, wheezed some more. The bitter metallic taste coated her tongue, seared her throat and chest, bringing sudden tears to her eyes.

A small price for freedom.

Her respiration returned to her in slow degrees. Not yet normal, but close. She should know by now not to wander around in the woods, or allow a sinfully, sexy doctor to kiss her.

"Brooke, is that you?" came from the bedroom.

Wonderful. All she needed was her mother's concern.

After shrugging off her flannel shirt and tossing it aside, Brooke collapsed onto the sofa. She glanced at the clock and wondered why her mother was still here. Of course, she knew. Jeanie Lewis had spent her life making Brooke's surroundings as sterile as possible. No annoying dust, no detrimental foods, nothing that held even the slightest possibility of aggravating Brooke's allergies and asthma. And Brooke hated it.

When Brooke could regain her voice, she called, "Yeah, Mom." She paused for a breath. "It's me."

"Good, dear. There's some vegetable pasta in the fridge. I threw out that carton of chocolate milk. You know better with your allergies."

Brooke decided that a morning trip to the convenience store to restock was now in order. "Okay, Mom."

"I'm just finishing up cleaning your blinds. I'll be out in a minute, then I need to get home to your father."

"Great, Mom." Another deeper breath. "Thanks."

Brooke allowed her mother these few concessions, cleaning the apartment like a maniac on a weekly basis, her attempts to control Brooke's diet, because it made Jeanie feel better and Brooke's life easier. It helped ease Jeanie's guilt for passing on a disease— a disease that had plagued her own mother—to her middle daughter.

Brooke rested her head against the back of the sofa and took in a few more easy breaths. The click of the front door lock drew her attention. Wonder of wonders. Her sister was home early for a change.

Michelle closed the door none too gently and tossed her purse onto the floor before sprawling into the lounge chair. She stretched out her legs and slumped down, ignoring the fact she wore a tight black dress. "That was sheer torture." Her eyelids dropped shut and she sighed.

Brooke tried to repress her smile. "Another unsuccessful foray into the dating world?"

Michelle slapped a palm to her forehead. "That's the understatement of the year. I swear I'm going to give up."

"Well, heaven help us, Michelle Lewis is giving up on men. Someone call the convent."

Michelle's eyes snapped open, and she stared at Brooke, first with annoyance, then with concern. "Lord, Brooke, you look terrible and you sound even worse."

"Shh. I'm fine." Brooke hooked a thumb over her shoulder. "Mom's here. She's scrubbing the blinds in the tub."

Michelle rolled her eyes to the ceiling. "Didn't she just do that last week?"

"Yes, but you know how those dust devils are. Persistent little beggars, I tell you. Worse than a used-car salesman."

Michelle clamped a hand over her mouth to muffle the giggles. Brooke didn't bother. She might not be able to live in comfortable disarray, but she was darn sure going to laugh when she felt like it. But laughing made her chest hurt.

After Michelle recovered, she asked, "So, how was your appointment with the doctor tonight?"

"You don't want to know."

Michelle came to attention. "Yes, I do."

Brooke didn't immediately respond. She liked playing this game. Make Michelle squirm.

Leaning forward, Michelle made a fist and held it up for Brooke's inspection. "Am I going to have to torture you?"

"You and who else, Miss Priss?"

Michelle scowled at the nickname even though it described her perfectly, at least from a physical standpoint. She'd always been the "pretty" one, tall and lithe where Brooke was short, more compact. She possessed long dark silky straight hair; Brooke's shoulder-length curly locks went out of control in high-humidity. Michelle's eyes were cut-glass blue; Brooke's were nothing-special brown.

Brooke admittedly had envied Michelle her assets on rare occasions. She had, more times, envied her sister's healthy lungs, a fact that sometimes shamed her senseless. Too often during their childhood, Brooke's medical problems had hindered the life of the "healthy" kid.

We can't go on vacation because Brooke's asthma is flaring up. We can't swim today because Brooke's a little short-winded.

Not once had Michelle complained. That didn't stop Brooke's occasional bouts of guilt. Still, Michelle was a rock. Heck, an immovable boulder. Brooke's best friend.

They'd never hidden one solitary thing from each other, the reason why Brooke prepared to tell her oldest sister everything about the recent events. "Something happened tonight."

Michelle studied Brooke for a long moment and

then proclaimed, "He kissed you," in a simple statement of fact.

Had Michelle joined the Psychic Sisters Network? "How would you know that?"

"Whisker burn."

Brooke slapped a hand to her mouth. Why, oh why, had she inherited her mother's fair complexion? Why couldn't she have Michelle's olive skin? "Let's just hope Mom doesn't notice."

As if on cue, "Michelle, is that you?" came from the bedroom.

"No, Mom," Brooke responded before Michelle could open her mouth. "I'm talking to my imaginary playmate, Sven."

"Oh, Brooke, you're such a card." Jeanie laughed, high-pitched and piercing. "Shelly, did you find an apartment yet?"

Michelle engaged in more eye rolling. "No, Mother, I told you that last night. But I'm still searching."

Brooke gave her a sympathetic look and a pat on the arm. "You can stay here as long as you like. I know it's small, but what's mine is yours." She lowered her voice. "Take Mom, for instance. Please."

Michelle fell into another fit of giggles but came to like a drill sergeant when Jeanie entered the room. Their mother stopped in front of the sofa table and studied her surroundings. The Queen of Clean surveying her royal domain. "Much better."

Brooke lent her requisite approval by nodding. "Yeah, Mom. Really great." Clean as a hospital ward and just as sterile. She might as well live at work.

Jeanie braced her hands on her hips and gave her daughters a quick once-over. Looking for latent dust, Brooke decided.

"How about some hot tea?" Jeanie asked.

"Sure," Brooke and Michelle said in unison.

After Jeanie made her way to the pass-through kitchen, Michelle slumped in the chair in a definite show of bravado.

Not only was their mom a Martha Stewart wannabe, she was also the Posture Police commander. Still, Brooke loved her dearly, despite her flawed humanity. Or maybe it was because of it.

"So finish you're story," Michelle whispered. "I'm dying to know every detail. Were you playing spin the syringe?"

Brooke met Michelle's silly grin and lowered her voice, too. "This isn't funny. I'm his therapist, he's my patient. The treatment plan doesn't include swapping gum."

Michelle scooted forward in the chair. "Let's look at this logically, shall we? You're both consenting adults, so what's the real problem here? Is it your job or the fact that you really liked it?"

"I really liked it."

Michelle sat back with a resounding sigh. "At least one of us got lucky."

Brooke massaged her temples, feeling the onset of a skull-blasting headache. "I don't know if he's just trying to prove he's still a man, or if he's really attracted to me."

"Don't be silly. Of course he's attracted to you. Men like Jared Granger don't have to hit on women that don't turn them on. He could probably make a few calls and have at least ten females waiting on his doorstep.''

''True, but what if he just wants my body? It really could be only superficial, although I can't imagine that.''

''Oh, please.'' Michelle glared at her. ''Would you just stop that? Any man would be crazy not to want you. I mean, look at you. You're pretty. You're smart. You have a wonderful sibling. I'd say you're a prime example of an excellent gene pool.''

Except for the asthma, Brooke thought. She wondered if Michelle was thinking the same thing, too.

''I think you should just go for it,'' Michelle said. ''Engage in a little slap and tickle with the doctor. Just make sure you don't get tangled up in all the emotional mess.''

Brooke ran her fingers up and down the arm of the leather lounger, thinking about Jared Granger. Thinking about the way he touched her in so many different ways, and it wasn't simply about sex. She was drawn to his vulnerability that he tried to hide more often than not. Drawn to her need to help him get over his fears and onto the road to recovery. Drawn to the man, not the doctor.

''I can't just turn off those emotions, Shelly. Seeing him all the time, watching him get better, knowing that he really *wants* to get better now, has started to work on me.''

''Does he have a girlfriend?'' Michelle asked.

''As far as I know, he's never been married. He's in his midthirties and not in a serious relationship.

Which means he's probably not commitment material."

Michelle leaned over and touched Brooke's arm. "Brooke, like I told you before, this doesn't have to be forever after. This can be a temporary thing. An—"

"Affair? I'm not sure I can handle that."

"You can if you decided from the get-go that's all it's going to be."

"I don't think I can do that."

Michelle's impatient sigh signaled she was gearing up for her usual commentary on Brooke's desolate life. "Now I understand what Bran—"

"Don't say it."

"—Brandon did to your confidence, but it's time to get past that and move on."

Brooke flinched at the name, the remembrance of a man who had nearly destroyed her heart. "I am over him. But I'm just being careful where Jared Granger's concerned."

"Who's this Jared, dear hearts?" their mom called from the kitchen.

Brooke winced. She didn't want to explain that earlier in the evening a patient had put her in a lip lock. "Jared's Shelly's boyfriend," she blurted out. "A wrestler. Big guy. Likes to put her in a headlock when they have sex."

"That's nice, honey."

Michelle snatched up a plastic-covered pillow and tossed it at Brooke. Laughing, Brooke made a quick right-handed catch before it hit the intended target, her head.

Right-handed catch.

Brooke thought about Jared, how he might never regain full function of his hand, at least not without help. She thought about seeing him again. Touching him. Bathing him. Pleasant chills ran down the length of her spine.

"So what are you going to do?" Michelle sat poised for an answer. Brooke wasn't sure she had one.

"I don't know."

"When do you see him again?"

"Monday." Brooke spoke in a near whisper. "And get this. I'm supposed to help him take a bath."

Michelle grinned. "Well now, that could be interesting. Wonder if he has a nice duckie?"

Brooke laughed. "You are so bad."

"But you cherish me, anyway."

"Yeah, I do."

"Look at it this way, Brooke. You could drag him out of his slump by example alone. You've never let your physical limi—" Michelle stopped short. Never had she referred to Brooke's asthma as a limitation, no matter how limiting it had been, or could be.

"It's okay, Shelly," Brooke said. "I know what I am. I know what I have. You're right. It doesn't stop me from trying. But you didn't see him today. He's just so—" she sighed "—hard to resist."

Michelle's expression turned serious. "If you want my opinion—"

"I don't."

"You should just see where it goes from here. No one has to know." Michelle's eyes sparked with that double-dog-dare-you light. "Come on, Brooke Lewis. Live a little for a change. You know you want to."

Truth was, Brooke did want to stay involved with Jared Granger. Not only for the thrill of being in his company, but in hopes of saving him from falling farther into a black hole of despair, like she almost had at one time. Could she really do that and still stay objective, or was she just being a fool? Wouldn't be the first time, or the last.

"One more thing," Michelle said. "Is he as great looking up close as he is at a distance?"

Brooke smiled when she recalled Jared's crystal-blue eyes, his high-impact grin, his wonderful lips. "Better than great."

Better than any man had a right to be.

Six

——

"Let me try it again." Jared reached for the red foam ball, fighting frustration. Fighting the urge to reach for Brooke instead. But tonight she'd maintained a cool detachment. An all-business facade. Not that he blamed her.

They'd been at the therapy session for over an hour, and he'd barely managed to cling to his control. He hadn't meant to direct his anger at her, yet she had been his prime target.

He tried again to grip the ball tighter, but one finger still wouldn't cooperate. He was beginning to sweat with the effort, and his wrist ached like a son of a gun.

"I think that's enough for now," Brooke said, her dark brows drawn into a frown.

"I'm not done yet."

"Well I am. You're only making yourself tired. You've made a lot of progress over the past few weeks, so don't be so hard on yourself."

He slammed the ball against the kitchen door with all the force he could muster. Brooke watched its progress without uttering one word as it bounced then rolled across the floor. And that ticked Jared off royally.

Why didn't she say something, dammit? Why did she have to sit there so cool and collected? "Look, you're the one who told me I wasn't trying hard enough," he said. "Now I'm trying too hard? Make up your mind!"

She stood and retrieved the ball, put it back in the bag, then sat down again with her hands clasped before her like some monument to serenity. "Temper, temper, Dr. Granger."

He hated her tolerance. Hated his own impatience, but he couldn't seem to stop it. At times he felt as if his life still spiraled out of control, and he couldn't do a damn thing to prevent it from happening. "I'm not getting any better," he declared, realizing he sounded like an irritated Little League pitcher trying unsuccessfully to execute a curve ball.

She reached for his hand and began to work his fingers once again with long, soothing strokes. "Yes, you are. You're starting to flex your fingers, loosen those tendons. It's only a matter of time before—"

"I go nuts." He tugged his hand away.

"Before you start to realize that your hand is going to work for you again."

"Except for this." He held up his uncooperative pointer finger, a necessary appendage if he ever planned to hold a delicate instrument again. "What do you propose I do about that?"

She looked concerned. "Give it time."

"I'm running out of time."

"What's the hurry?"

He leaned forward. "What's the hurry? I want to go back to surgery. I need to go back. Doing nothing all the time is driving me insane."

"I understand that, but you can't rush this process. You can start going without the splint, though."

Glancing at the contraption sitting next to the discarded hot pack, he felt an overwhelming fear. A fear he didn't understand or welcome. "Are you sure I'm ready for that?"

"Yeah, I'm sure. You have enough mobility now so it's not necessary to wear it."

He sat in silence for a moment, pondering her suggestion. The damned thing had once been a thorn in his backside and now it served as a crutch. He'd never been dependent on anything or anyone. He didn't like it one bit.

Brooke touched his arm, garnering his attention, drawing him in with her dusky eyes. "I know it's kind of scary at first, but you'll see that it's okay—"

"I'm not scared, dammit." He protested too much and, by the compassionate look on Brooke's face, he figured she saw right through him. He wanted to kiss that compassion away. He wanted to do more than that. Right now his frustration resulted not only from the need to forget his predicament but also from a desire so great it made him want to take a few chances he probably shouldn't take. Instead he leaned back in his chair and studied Brooke's angelic face, wondering how far he should go. He knew how far he wanted this thing between them to go, but he doubted she would agree. At least not without some heavy-duty persuasion.

Only one way to find out. Actually, two, but he chose the less obvious one. "You ready to help me with my bath?"

She could not believe she was doing this.

Brooke stared at the claw-footed tub, the rubber stopper gripped in her hand so tightly it almost popped out several times. Jared Granger was in his bedroom, only a few feet away, undressing. Not that it should take too long. He was wearing a faded pair of blue scrubs tonight, as if he were preparing for surgery, or for bed.

Oh, heavens.

She didn't need to think about that now. Not when he was in the other room, probably totally naked, waiting for her to give him the signal she was ready for him. Ready for *him?* Yeah, right.

She had barely been able to concentrate on the therapy, her mind drifting into thoughts of what would come. He had been cooperative and considerate at first, using his smile to knock the rug out from under her hesitation. Then came the anger, the disillusionment. And the request for the bath. She had found herself agreeing, in part to soothe his frustration. In part because she had promised to help him. And now here she was, making good on that promise, probably at her own peril.

Brooke turned on the water and tested the temperature with one elbow, then slipped the stopper into place. Standing, she looked around the room, making sure she had everything on hand, including her professionalism. After all, it shouldn't be that difficult to get him into the tub as long as he kept the towel positioned where it would hide his assets.

Digging through her canvas bag, she pulled out the bottle of foaming peach-scented milk bath. Bubbles would certainly aid in screening things best left unseen.

Once the tub was full and foaming, she turned off the water and called, "I'm ready."

Hardly. She realized that fact the minute he appeared at the door, the navy towel slung low on his hips, reaching the top of his thighs. His well-defined chest was bare as well as the foot not covered by the cast. Did she really believe he'd be wearing shoes and shirt, as if this were a restaurant, not a bathroom?

She had to get her mind in the right gear if she was ever going to get through this. How could she when he stood there with one hip cocked against the door frame and a come-and-get-me look on his face?

Shoring up her courage, she stood in front of the toilet and said, "Okay, let's see how this is going to work, shall we?"

"I'm game." He hobbled toward the tub, and she turned sideways to allow him room. They faced each other, and Brooke suddenly realized the bath was no bigger than the playhouse her dad had built for her seventh birthday. Back then all she'd needed was enough room for Barbie and Ken, a practically androgynous couple, aside from their fancy wardrobe. Back then all she wanted to do was play make-believe. Back then she sure didn't imagine bathing a devastating doctor who radiated sexuality like a halogen bulb.

The air was heavy with the scent of peaches and masculine musk. Brooke's heart rate accelerated to accommodate her rapid breathing, her sprinting pulse.

Jared sent a pointed look at the tub now nearly overflowing. "Bubbles?" He shot her a less-than-happy glance. "Bubbles?" he repeated.

"Yes, bubbles. I find them very soothing." If only she'd had a good soak first, then maybe she wouldn't be wound as tightly as an old-fashioned alarm clock.

"I really don't care to smell like fruit," he growled.

"You'll just have to deal with it. I'm not rerunning the water—unless you want to take a cold bath, because I doubt you have any hot water left."

"Maybe a cold bath's not such a bad idea. It's supposed to ease certain urges."

Don't look, Brooke. But darned if she didn't look, straight at the towel barely covering his manly attributes. And what a sight to behold.

Oh, good grief. She was acting like some sex-starved kitten, ready to purr and pounce.

Averting her gaze from the very obvious bulge in the terry, she said, "Since we need to keep your left leg up, you'll have to face the faucet."

"Fine."

She moved beside him, but not before brushing up against all that maleness.

Meow.

Get a hold of yourself, Brookie. Better her than him.

She swallowed hard as if she could really choke

down the wicked thoughts. "Put your arm around my neck, then step over the tub."

He reached for the knotted towel.

"Don't take that off!" My gosh, had she really sounded that loud?

He gave her a crooked smile. "What's the matter? Afraid you'll go blind?"

No, she was afraid she wouldn't. "I meant just leave it on and once you're in, then you can take it off."

"Come on, Brooke. You're not shy, are you?"

The husky tone of his voice made her shiver. "If you must know…yes, I am."

"Funny, I didn't take you for the modest type, since you're in the medical field. I mean, hey, you've seen one, you've seen 'em all."

Boy, was he ever wrong. "Just get in the tub. I've got a good grip on you."

"Don't I wish."

Ignoring the innuendo, she grasped his hand and braced herself while he lifted his right leg into the tub. She bent and helped him ease into the water as she lifted his left leg and rested it along the ledge. All the while she managed to focus on the faucet instead of the towel.

Thank heavens they'd gotten this far without disturbing her delicate sensibilities, which were anything but delicate at the moment.

The slap of wet terry at her feet startled her, so much so that she dropped his arm from around her neck and stepped back. Thank goodness it wasn't his bad hand that hit the ledge. Her gaze immediately shot to where the towel should have been, and she praised Barney Bubble, or whomever it was that had invented suds.

Drawing a cleansing breath, she reached for the bar of soap from the dish mounted to the wall and offered it to him. "Here. Have fun."

"Mind washing my back?"

Mind administering CPR? "Okay, I guess I can do that."

He leaned forward and she moved to her knees behind the tub, immediately behind him.

When he leaned forward, giving her access to his back, she tried hard not to notice details. She tried hard to think of it as an inanimate object. Obviously she wasn't trying hard enough. She noticed everything. The smooth surface all the way down to where the water met his waist. The solid track of his perfect spine. The small whitish scar beneath his shoulder blade and another at his left rib cage.

She imagined he tanned well in the summer, and with that golden hair to match his golden skin, he probably resembled a surfer. She'd be better off imagining him as a surfboard.

With both hands on the bar of soap, she maintained a good grip, fearing it might squirm from her fingertips and into the water. No way would she go looking for it. No telling what she might find.

Brooke worked the soap into a lather, moving the bar up and down the bumpy pearls of his spine, across his broad shoulders, down to his trim waist but not daring to go farther. Not that she wouldn't like to. Actually, she would like to. Very, very much.

"Are *you* having fun?"

Yes, as a matter of fact, she was. More fun than should be legally allowed. "Why do you ask?"

"Because you're going to rub a hole in my back if you keep it up."

Her face lit up like a campfire. "Sorry." She stood and again offered him the soap. "It's all yours."

His smile came full force. "Mind washing my—"

"Yes, I do mind."

"I was going to say my hair."

"Oh."

His wily grin deepened. "What did you think I was going to say?"

"Never mind." She impatiently tapped her foot. "You can't manage washing your hair?"

"Guess I could, but it gets cleaner if done with two good hands."

He had a point, darn him. "I'll go get a cup from the kitchen."

"Promise not to drown me? Mona almost did the other day."

"Who's Mona?" Did she really want to know?

"My housekeeper. Mona the maid."

Annoyingly that relieved Brooke. "Does she wear one of those little French numbers and carry a feather duster?"

"No. She dresses in drab gray and wields a mean vacuum. She's in her sixties. A German woman with steel fingers and a grip like a sailor. She made me stand over the sink while she scrubbed my scalp until I thought I'd go bald before she was done."

"What did you do to provoke her?"

"Not a thing. She's into torture."

"How nice." She tossed the bar of soap into the

tub where it landed near a strategic area on Jared's person.

"Sure wish you hadn't done that," he said. "Hard to pick up a bar of soap with one good hand. Want to help?"

Yes, she did, but she didn't dare. "I'm sure you'll manage."

He rubbed a hand over his square jaw. "Just for the record, I'm not into the rough stuff. I prefer slow and easy. Taking my time. All night—"

Brooke couldn't get to the door fast enough in hope of escaping Jared Granger's sensuality and her sudden carnal cravings. Escaping the urge to run her fingers down the silky mat of chest hair and lower still, right where the soap had landed.

"Hurry back." His gruff laughter followed her all the way out the door.

Jared wouldn't be a bit surprised if Brooke kept going, past the kitchen and out the front door. He wouldn't be a bit surprised if she just left him there with his bum leg suspended over the ledge and his body shriveling up like a prune.

One part of him would probably still remain unaffected, even after spending days in tepid water. No chance it would be shriveling anytime soon, at least not with the prospect of Brooke's return hanging over him.

Grabbing the rag draped over the side of the tub, he began scrubbing his face, behind his ears, down his chest, and onto his privates. What a shame that he couldn't convince her to help him out with that. But he wasn't a fool. He'd already pushed her to the limit, that much he knew, although she hadn't seemed to mind touching him. He sure as hell hadn't minded.

He'd been up for this bath since the moment she'd agreed to help him. He was still up for it. Completely.

After a few minutes Brooke returned with a basin tucked underneath her arm, a small stool underneath the other and a plastic cup gripped in her hand. Jared released the breath he'd been holding, thankful she hadn't run out on him, which pleased him in more ways than one.

She put the stool down behind the tub and the basin sideways in the sink. After pushing up the sleeves on her baggy shirt, she reconsidered and shucked it off her slim shoulders, leaving her clad in a blue knit top that barely covered her midriff. Jared glimpsed the pale flesh at her belly and the crease of her navel before she tugged the hem down to cover herself.

Damn.

Going back to the sink, she began to fill the basin. "Looks like you do still have some hot water."

"I've got an adequate heater."

"Do you, now?" She sent him a smile.

He couldn't resist the urge to tease her any more than he could resist her. "Yeah. It works really well, even under pressure."

"I imagine it does." She brought the basin and cup to rest on the stool behind him. "Hold your breath. I'm about to anoint you."

Jared closed his eyes and braced for the baptism. The water only came in a small trickle down his forehead, not the sudden rush of water he'd expected. No surprise she could do this as well as she had done everything else. And he wouldn't be at all surprised to know she did *everything* well. That thought raised the flag from half-mast to full glory. Lucky for her the bubbles were still intact. Unlucky for him, so was his white-hot need.

After she had his scalp sufficiently soaked, she worked her way to the side of the tub and reached for the shampoo from the holder. Her breasts brushed across his chest, and it was all he could do not to groan. She didn't seem to notice, or at least she pretended not to.

With gentle fingertips she massaged the shampoo into his hair, working his scalp with firm yet steady strokes, just as she'd worked his stiff fingers earlier. He closed his eyes and imagined her fingers elsewhere, stroking him straight into oblivion. He balanced on the edge of control, ready to give everything over to impulse.

She removed her great hands and began rinsing the shampoo away, every now and then slicking his hair back from his forehead. In the midst of one of those forays, he grasped her wrist and gave her arm a tug.

"Come here," he said, his voice harsh with unsuppressed desire.

Amazingly she scooted around to the side of the tub and regarded him with concern. "Did I get soap in your eyes?"

"Lady, you've done a lot more than that." He circled her nape with his left hand and pulled her to him. He kissed her with an urgency he couldn't restrain, not waiting to see if she protested. Her lips parted, and he claimed her mouth as if he had the right. She began to work more magic with her tongue, touching it to his in a steady rhythm reminiscent of the first time he'd kissed her. Now he wanted more of what she could give him. What she *would* give him.

Breaking the kiss, she pulled back but not completely away. "I'm getting wet."

Jared wouldn't be at all shocked if the water began to boil. "That's the idea."

She looked down at her chest where the bubbles had formed two perfect peaks at her breasts. Jared took the opportunity to thumb one mound away. Her nipple hardened beneath his fingertip as he brushed over the moisture. He cursed the fact his other hand didn't work the way it should.

She didn't seem to mind his one-handed effort, evident by the way her eyes drifted closed and her bottom lip quivered as if she'd escaped into some erotic world. He watched her face go soft, then watched his hand circle her breast while she sat on her knees, perfectly still, and let him do what he had wanted to do for what seemed like forever.

He managed to lift her shirt, exposing the sheer white bra that left little to his imagination. The dark circles showing beneath the fabric made his mouth water with the urge to taste her. He leaned forward and took one nipple into his mouth through the fabric, brushing his tongue back and forth, wanting to experience the warmth of her flesh without anything standing in the way, especially a functional white bra.

She moaned softly, driving him to the brink. He couldn't remember the last time he was so hard, so needy. Nor could he remember the last time he'd heard anything so sweet, or known anyone so tempting as Brooke Lewis.

"Jared..."

His name leaving her lips sent deep satisfaction washing over him. "Say it again."

Her eyes blinked open, filled with surprise. "What?"

"I want to hear you say my name again."

She sat back on her haunches. "Is that what I said?"

He couldn't help but smile. "Yeah. You said Jared. My name. Not Dr. Granger."

"Oh, no."

Why hadn't he left well enough alone?

She slowly stood and pulled her shirt back into place, swiping at her breasts as if she could remove the moisture either from the bubbles or where his mouth had been.

"I think we're all done here," she said, looking away.

No, they weren't, but he would play along. For now. "Are you going to help me out?"

She finally looked at him. "Of the tub?"

"Yeah. That, too."

She groaned and muttered what he thought to be a string of curses directed at him. "Let me get a towel. Don't move."

Walking to the linen closet, she reached up to the top shelf, giving him a good view of the dip of her spine and the creamy flesh at her back where the shirt rode up right above her great butt. A nice spot to kiss, he decided. If she let him. And she would one day, whether she cared to acknowledge that fact or not. At least she hadn't run out on him. Yet.

Coming back with the towel, she slapped it to his chest and said, "Hold this." Then she crouched down and pulled his arm around her neck. With a little maneuvering, she helped him up. Out of respect for her, he managed to hold the towel and hide his sins. Not that they weren't obvious even with the towel.

Once his cast hit the tiled floor, Jared started to slide. Brooke grabbed him around the waist and tried to stop his forward momentum. Somehow they ended up with her back to the wall and him leaning into her. Completely flush against her. And somewhere along the way he'd lost the towel.

He braced his left hand above her head, trapping her between him and the wall. If he were a gentleman, he'd back off. At the moment he didn't feel at all gentlemanly. His need was feral. Untamed. He wanted her to know exactly what she was doing to him and what he intended for her, if she would only give him the chance.

Brooke braced her hands against Jared's chest, thinking she should shove him back. She truly should. But his nearness, his heat, drew on her feminine center like bees to pollen. Her whole body flooded with heat, from the top of her head to between her thighs.

Jared's lips rested against her ear. "This is quite a predicament we have here."

He could say that again. His obvious *predicament* was sending her brain into a tailspin, taking all her protests with it. "Yes, it is."

"What do you think we should do about it?"

"Beats me." She hadn't even realized until that moment she was running her fingertips through the mat of hair on his chest like some foraging animal. She felt like an animal.

He kissed her then, committing his whole mouth to

hers. His left hand came up to again caress her breast, and all the fight seeped out of her, as if she really intended to fight him at all. Deep down she had wanted this, no matter how logical the arguments against it. He probably knew that, and maybe he was taking supreme advantage, but right now she was a willing participant in this dangerous game.

Slowly he slid his hand downward, over her belly and lower until he cupped her between her thighs. A sound seeped out of her parted lips, foreign to her ears and mouth. So were the building sensations as he continued to stroke her through the denim. The friction felt delicious, although she wanted all obstacles gone. She wanted to feel his hands touching her in places she'd never been touched before. Not by Brandon. Not by any man.

This was so insane. So unfathomable that she would let him do this. A patient, no less. A doctor. Where was her good sense? Shredded to bits by Jared Granger's skilled hands.

"Do you know how long I've imagined this?" he whispered.

She shook her head, unable to form intelligible words.

"Probably since the day I met you. But not like this."

He tried to move his hand away, but Brooke wouldn't let him. She had become someone else in that moment. A wild, needy woman who cared only about this man's touch.

"Brooke, let me take you to bed. Do this right."

He was doing fine, as far as she was concerned. Despite his suggestion he still continued to stroke her and in just the right spot. He applied sudden pressure with the heel of his hand, abruptly sending her over the edge with a climax that shook her to the core. Her knees began to buckle, but he was there, holding her up as she trembled in his arms until the waves subsided.

The euphoria lifted and mortification took its place. What did he think of her now? She didn't want to know.

Gentle fingers tipped her chin up, and she met his dark gaze. "Are you okay?"

She lowered her eyes and noted he wasn't at all okay. He was completely aroused. She tore her eyes away and brought her gaze back to his face. "No, I'm not all right. I'm nuts. I'm a fool. And I quit."

Ducking under his arm, she headed toward the door.

"Brooke, wait."

She at least owed him an explanation, but she was afraid to face him. After all, he didn't have on a stitch of clothes, and she would bet her paycheck he was still cocked and ready for action. Her fault, too. Did that make her the ultimate tease?

The least she could do was apologize for her careless behavior. Deciding it was time to grow up and get with the program, she turned. Fortunately he had somehow managed to pick up the towel and drape it back into place.

"Don't go," he said.

"I have to go. We shouldn't be doing this."

He limped toward her. "Look, if you think I expect more from you, I don't. You're not ready. I realize that now. But I don't want you to quit. I still need you."

Oh, brother. There he went with that *need* thing again. Just another reminder of why she couldn't continue to work with Jared Granger. Kiss Jared Granger. Touch Jared Granger.

"I'll find someone else to help you out."

His expression went stern, angry. "I don't want anyone else. I want you. All of you. Not just the damned therapy. I want more than that. And when you're ready, I want it all."

Would she ever be ready for that? Could she trust herself enough to enjoy only the moment and walk away when the moment was gone? "I can't even think about that now."

He managed another slow smile. "When I want something bad enough, like you, I usually get it."

Damn his persistence. "I'll let Dr. Kempner know I'm resigning as your therapist."

"You don't have to. You're fired."

Her eyes widened. "What?"

"You heard me. You're fired. Then we don't have to worry about ethics or any of that garbage. We'll be free to do as we please, and, babe, my main goal is to please you."

He already had. But that wasn't the point. "No one has ever fired me before."

"There's always a first for everything." He took another step forward and brushed a lock of hair away from her cheek. "And as far as you and I are concerned, this is going to be one first you won't want to miss."

If she stayed any longer, she'd fall back into his arms and probably into his bed. "I have to go."

He made a sweeping gesture toward the door behind her. "Then go. I'll call you tomorrow."

"I don't think—"

For a man with a broken leg, he certainly moved fast. He was on her like a duck on a June bug before she realized what was happening. And he was kissing her, stealing her breath, robbing her resolve, making her want him more.

The kiss didn't last nearly long enough, before he put some distance between them. "You can go now, but remember one thing. I'm not going away."

Seven

"**B**rooke, you have a phone call."

Brooke glanced up from her patient to her boss standing at the door looking expectant.

Already running behind today, Brooke didn't have the time or desire to chat. "Can I call them back?"

Macy opened the door a little wider. "It's Dr. Granger. He says it's important."

Her heart did a rat-a-tat-tat in her chest. She couldn't very well refuse his call without rousing Macy's suspicions. "Okay. I'll take it in the break room."

"Fine. Line four."

After Macy disappeared, Brooke took a deep breath and patted Mrs. Moore on the arm, a nice lady with a sore neck and a cheerful disposition. If only all her patients were this pleasant. "I'm sorry. This shouldn't take too long. I'll be right back."

Mrs. Moore gave her a winning smile. "That's okay, dear. I know how those doctors can be."

Not this one, Brooke thought as she left the room.

Once in the hall she hurried into the break room, thankful to find she was alone. Her hands trembled as she grabbed for the receiver from the wall phone and pushed the flashing red line. "Hello?"

"Took you long enough."

Not the greeting she'd expected, but then when had he done anything she'd expected? "I happen to be working. In fact, I've left someone literally hanging, so I only have a few moments."

"Oh, so now you're into hanging patients."

"It's traction."

"Good. You had me worried. I'll make this quick."

She doubted that. "So what can I do for you today, Dr. Granger? If I recall, you fired me last night." Among other things.

"I want to see you tonight."

Brooke bit her bottom lip, almost hard enough to yelp. "I'm supposed to have a birthday dinner with my family."

"Whose birthday?"

Did she dare tell him something so personal? Oh, why not. They'd been up close and personal last night. "Mine."

"Why didn't you say something?"

"Because it's no big deal."

"It is to me."

Why was he doing this? Why was he speaking in *that* voice—smooth and warm going down like expensive scotch? "Well, it's just another day to me, but I'm afraid my family feels this need to celebrate."

"What time do you have to be there?"

"Eight."

"Then meet me before. At six on the Riverwalk. Neutral territory. We can have drinks."

"I don't know if that's such a great idea. You're mighty dangerous around water *without* the benefit of alcohol."

His throaty chuckle traveled all the way from her ear to her soul. "I promise I won't toss you in, unless you want to go skinny-dipping. That could be interesting."

Now her thoughts had really run amok, whirling back to last night and her shameless behavior. She chafed her arms with her hands, wondering what the heck was wrong with the thermostat. She went from chilled to hot to chilled again. "I think leaving our clothes on would be best since it is November."

His heavy sigh filtered through the line. "Spoilsport. But if you don't want to swim, then we can at least take a walk. I'm itching to try out my leg now that the cast is off."

"So they did take it off?" She couldn't contain her excitement, and that irritated her. She shouldn't be concerned with his leg, or any other part of him. But she was. All of his parts, as a matter of fact. She looked around to make sure no one was present to witness her blush.

"Yeah, I can walk almost normally again," he said. "Might be nice for us to celebrate my emancipated leg and your birthday."

How could she refuse him? She should, but she

couldn't. Besides, they did need to set things straight. "Where do you want me to meet you?"

"In front of the entrance of the River Center. There's a few tables set up outside not far from the food court."

"I know the place. But make it six-thirty. That way I'll have time to go home and change clothes."

"We could make clothes optional."

Obviously, he was determined to keep her off balance. "Are you going to behave yourself?"

"If I must."

"Then I'll see you at six-thirty."

"That doesn't give us much time. Are you sure you can't make it by six?"

She could, but if she wanted to be strong, she needed less time in the presence of all his tempting talk and drop dead grin. "Six-thirty," she stated firmly. "And just one more thing. No gifts."

"Well, since you probably don't consider my company a gift, I guess we're safe there."

If he only knew. Spending time with Jared Granger was the best present she could ever give herself. And a most dangerous one. "I'll see you then."

"I'm looking forward to it," he said, and hung up.

Brooke dropped the phone back into its cradle. What was she doing? Taking a huge chance, she decided. Maybe Michelle was right. Maybe it was time to take a chance.

"What did Dr. Granger want, Brooke?"

Brooke turned to find her boss leaning back against the cabinet, sprigs of salt-and-pepper hair falling at will from her low ponytail as if she'd just left a wind tunnel—and suspicion written all over her plump face.

Brooke had planned to talk to Macy about discontinuing Jared's therapy. Now seemed as good a time as any. "Actually, Dr. Granger has dismissed me."

Macy braced a hand on her thick waist and frowned. "I assume the home therapy didn't work out."

Yes, and no, Brooke thought, trying not to smile at the memories. "He's made quite a bit of progress, so it wasn't all a wash." Except for the bath.

"What does he intend to do now?"

Brooke wished she knew. "I'm not sure. He may be developing a contracture in one digit. Surgery could be in his future."

Macy's eyes narrowed. "Did you tell him about your suspicions?"

No, she hadn't. But she would eventually. Maybe even tonight. "I didn't want to discourage him. I thought he could use a little more time."

"Do you really think that was wise?"

"I think it was the best under the circumstances. He might take it better coming from Dr. Kempner instead of me."

"Did you try to persuade him to continue therapy until that determination can be made?"

Macy had no earthly idea how much persuasion had taken place, but not the PT kind. "I encouraged him to continue," Brooke said. "I guess we'll have to wait and see what he does."

Macy turned to go, then faced Brooke again with a questioning look. "Are you telling me everything?"

Sudden panic weighted Brooke's chest, hindering her breathing. "I'm not sure what you mean."

"Did something happen between you two?"

Brooke bit back the urge to laugh hysterically. "Macy, Dr. Granger is an expert physician." An expert at everything, she imagined. "I'm sure he knows what he's doing." Very sure.

Macy didn't looked at all convinced. Not surprising to Brooke. "Have you notified Dr. Kempner of his decision?"

"Dr. Granger said he'd do it." Another lie. They hadn't discussed what would happen next with the therapy, or their personal relationship.

"Well, be sure to make a note in his chart and then follow up with Dr. Kempner."

"I will."

Macy pushed her glasses up the bridge of her nose and eyed Brooke warily. "Brooke, you're one of the most compassionate therapists we have on staff. That can be very good or very bad in some instances."

Brooke felt steady heat flow to her face and cursed her carelessness. She suspected Macy had overheard some of the conversation with Jared. "What are you saying?"

"Sometimes the lines in the patient-therapist relationship blur. I'd hate to see you get hurt because of it."

Brooke managed a smile. "Don't worry, Macy. I'm fine."

Macy returned her smile with a knowing one. "And so, my dear, is Dr. Granger."

With that, Macy swayed out the door, her ample hips keeping time with her sassy gait.

Brooke closed her eyes and inhaled, then exhaled slowly. The image of Jared burned behind her closed lids.

She opened her eyes, hoping his face would just go away so she could get on with work. It didn't. He was with her 24/7 every day now, even jumping into her dreams at night.

Macy's caution came back to her. *I'd hate to see you get hurt.* Brooke's biggest fear.

She was no longer Jared's therapist. No longer tied to him by a professional relationship. But she was still tied to him on a much deeper level. A personal level. Was she setting herself up for another fall?

All she could do was take it one day at time, beginning with tonight.

San Antonio was supercharged with sensuality. Brooke had lived in the place most of her life, but she'd never seen the sights with a man. Until tonight.

As she approached the commons area positioned near the end of one finger of the river, her senses were tuned to the sounds of muffled conversations, the smells of spicy foods and fresh-baked tortillas. She had been there often to shop at the riverfront stores, always taking the atmosphere for granted. Tonight she noticed all the little things, the subtle details, including lovers strolling hand in hand along the walkway.

Then she noticed him. A lone man with his back to her, facing the river.

He wore a navy blazer and khaki slacks, his hair recently trimmed away from his nape. His right hand was hidden away in a pocket, the other, she assumed, braced on the railing in front of him. His towering height, broad shoulders and long legs made him appear all-powerful, imposing, providing a perfect backdrop to the shops bedecked with twinkling lights in preparation for Christmas even though Thanksgiving was still two weeks away.

The doctor incarnate had returned.

Brooke wished for a camera to capture his shadowy figure set against the near-night sky like some beautiful fallen archangel. She paused simply to stare, before he was aware she watched him, biding her time to get her heart and respiration under control before she faced him once again.

As if he sensed her perusal, he slowly turned. He greeted her with a half smile and a single red rose.

She carefully descended the steps and moved onto the narrow walkway separating them, careful not to turn her ankle in the two-inch heels she'd foolishly decided to wear.

"I thought I told you no gifts," she said in a mock-serious tone.

"How do you know I didn't buy this for me?" His eyes reflected mischief of the most lethal kind. The kind that could get a girl into serious trouble should she succumb.

She smiled. "Oh, well then, my apologies. Looks nice with your jacket."

He ran the petals of the rose across her cheek, making her breath hitch hard in her chest. "I couldn't very well come empty-handed, knowing it's your birthday."

She took the flower and drew in its fragrance, second only to the scent of Jared's mellow woodsy cologne wafting on the slight breeze. "I suppose I should say you shouldn't have, but I'm really glad you did.''

His smile expanded, lighting up his eyes. Lighting up her heart. ''No trouble at all. I picked it up from a vendor. Not very original, I guess, but my options were limited on such short notice.''

''It's beautiful. I haven't had one in a long time.''

His breathtaking smile of satisfaction did things to Brooke she'd never experienced before. ''That's too bad.''

''Actually, I'm allergic to them.''

He looked alarmed. ''You are?''

Brooke couldn't stop her laughter. She felt such freedom. Such wild abandon. ''No. I'm kidding. And I'm sorry. A mean trick.''

He inclined his head and narrowed his eyes. ''You've got a little devil in you, don't you, Brooke Lewis?''

Right now she was feeling more than a little devilish. ''At times, yes.''

''Do you want to have that drink now?''

Brooke's rumbling stomach reacted to the nearby restaurant smells, reminding her she hadn't had a real lunch. ''I haven't eaten much today. Just a few crackers. If I have even the least bit of alcohol, it will go straight to my head.'' And at the moment she was feeling quite dizzy without the help of a margarita, thanks to the doctor.

''I know what you mean,'' he said. ''Just seeing you all dressed up is giving me one helluva rush.''

Brooke smoothed her hand down the winter-white jacket covering the matching skirt. She fought off the resulting blush, the need to protest and say, Why, this old thing? Her mother's admonitions came back to her. *Always take a compliment with grace.* So Brooke simply said, "Thank you. You clean up good, too."

He rubbed his neck. "I actually went home tonight and took a shower. I even got my hair cut before my appointment. I thought it was high time to rejoin the real world, not that I don't prefer jeans and T-shirts."

Brooke preferred him any way he wanted to be— repressed farmer or revered doctor. "Why don't we take a walk? Act like tourists." Being in public seemed marginally safe.

He made a sweeping gesture toward the cement walkway running alongside the small river. "Let's go."

She moved to his left side before he stopped her by taking her shoulders and moving her to his right. "Let me walk over here on the outside."

"Why?"

"In case some passerby decides to get fresh with you. With that outfit, anything's possible."

She felt light-headed, giddy, totally taken in by his charm. "How chivalrous, Dr. Granger."

He stopped and faced her. "It's Jared. Tonight we're two people enjoying each other's company. I don't think the ethics police are standing by waiting to hear you call me by my first name. Besides, I'm no longer your patient. Remember?"

How could she forget? "Okay… *Jared.* Happy now?"

"I'm working on it."

They walked in silence for a few moments, the comfortable quiet interrupted now and then when they passed a particularly rowdy restaurant or club, noisy revelry filtering through the open doors and outdoor patios.

"So you're joining your family for dinner," Jared finally said.

Brooke frowned at the thought. "Yes, the usual togetherness. Mom fussing over me like I'm ten, my dad fidgeting so he can get back to the game of the week. Michelle arguing with my mom over why she hasn't found a nice man and settled down."

"You're mom doesn't bug you about that?"

"Not about finding a husband and starting a family, no."

"Why's that?"

Boy, this could get complicated. "Mainly because of the asthma, I think, although she's never admitted that to me. I was pretty sick as a kid, and she's made it her life's work to try and keep me sheltered from the world, and in a way dependent on her, I guess. I just let her think that's what she's doing and go on about my business."

"So she's worried that you'll pass the asthma on."

"Yes. Her mother had it and died fairly young."

"But that must've been some time ago. Medicine's made a lot of advancements in treatment in recent years."

"Yes, but Mom deals in guilt. She's an expert." Brooke glanced at Jared and caught his smile surfacing. "Is that funny?"

"No, just familiar."

She laid a dramatic hand on her chest. "Don't tell me, your parents are guilt experts, too?"

"My dad can dole it out, although he's more subtle. I've been in training to be a doctor from day one.

Groomed to carry on the tradition. It was expected of me. God only knows what would've happened if I'd decided to do something else, like become a paratrooper, which I actually considered during my rebellious days.''

Brooke could just picture it. G.I. Jared. ''So your dad was a doctor?''

''Yeah, him and his dad. The very best.''

''And that's what drives you.''

He sent her a look of surprise, as if he didn't expect her insight. ''Yeah, that and the fact I don't see myself doing anything else or really enjoying anything else.''

''I'd say you've carried on the legacy well. I've always considered you the best in the city. Probably even the state.''

He took a sudden turn left onto a bridge arcing over the water and stopped to lean forward against the rock wall.

''Is your leg bothering you?'' she asked, coming to his side.

''Not much. I thought we might want to stop for a while.''

She wasn't sure if he meant stop walking or stop the thread of conversation about his life. Silence stretched between them as they stood shoulder to shoulder, surveying the surroundings from a different vantage point. More than ever, Brooke was aware of him as a man. A real flesh-and-blood man with feelings and vulnerabilities not unlike her own. A man highly regarded by the medical community. A man who had almost lost everything.

"I need to explain about last night," he said, turning to face her.

Brooke's cheeks flamed at the thought of what he'd done to her. How quickly she had responded to a few simple touches. "Let's just say it was one of those things, and leave it at that."

"I can't leave it at that."

He stared off in the distance for a moment before turning his attention back to her. "When I really want something, I usually jump in with both feet. No hesitation, just grab for the gusto. It's something I've learned, and I haven't been able to change it. I haven't wanted to change until now. Until I met you."

Her heart fluttered like a hummingbird's wings. "I wouldn't want you to change because of me. I admire your tenacity."

"But last night I had you at an unfair advantage. I've known all along that you're not comfortable with this relationship, and I pushed you. But I'm willing to try anything to change your mind about us."

Her mind had been changing little by little, with every kiss, everything he had revealed about himself. "Look, Jared, I'm a big girl. I could have stopped you. I didn't want to." There. She said it, and it wasn't as difficult as she'd assumed.

His smile was pure satisfaction. "You really mean that?"

"Yes, I really mean that. If I had felt at all threatened, I would've gone for the mace and baseball bat, and you wouldn't have known what hit you."

He tilted his face toward the star-spattered sky and laughed. A rich, deep sound that rumbled low in his chest. "Now why doesn't that surprise me?"

"Because I think you know me better than you realize." Better than she had ever intended.

Taking both her hands into his, he said, "I want to know you even better."

"We'll see." It was the only promise she could make at the moment, still afraid that she might be making a mistake. But temptation was beginning to outweigh emotional safety.

"Have you ever been on one of those things?" He nodded toward a river taxi passing underneath the bridge.

"Only once when I was in a hurry. Just to get from one point to the next. I've never been on the entire trip."

"Want to try it?"

Brooke shrugged. "Sure. Why not? Might be fun."

Taking her by surprise, he squeezed her hands. With both hands, including his injured one. Not a solid grip, yet enough to signal his fingers were returning to normal. All except one.

Should she tell him now about her suspicions? No. She didn't care to shatter his good mood. Later. Much later.

Once Jared purchased the tickets, they only had to wait a few moments for the taxi to arrive. He clasped her hand again and helped her onto the flat-bottomed boat. They took a bench seat near the rear, away from the pilot. A couple with two young children was the only party present on the boat. At the next stop, the family departed, leaving Brooke and Jared alone.

As the boat pulled away from the bank, Jared draped his arm over her shoulder and tugged her close against his side. A few days ago she would have protested, tried to maintain some distance between them. But he was quickly closing her self-imposed gap with every move he made, including this one.

She found herself relaxing even more as he traced a path up and down her arm, back and forth, with a satin caress that seemed timed with the steady sway of the boat. Even through the thick fabric of the jacket, she wasn't unaffected by his random touch. The nippy breeze dancing across her face did nothing to cool her. Every movement of Jared's strong fingertips brought her closer to a place she had no business going. A place of desire filled with an overwhelming need for this man.

Maybe it was only the romantic ambience, or Jared's cologne. Or the fact that she'd never done this before. Or maybe it was simply him, his presence. The man beneath the doctor. A man she admired more than she ever thought possible.

When she shivered, he whispered, "Are you cold?"

On the contrary, she was very warm. "A little."

He sat forward, taking his heat with him, then removed his jacket and placed it over her like a blanket. "Is that better?"

"Mmm-hmm," she murmured, although in reality she craved his nearness, his heat, his touch. That would be better.

As if he'd read her thoughts, again he draped his arm around her, only this time he turned slightly to the side and slipped his free arm underneath the jacket, bringing it to rest over her abdomen, his hand immediately below her rib cage.

She rested her head against his shoulder, feeling

drugged. Totally limp with longing. Every nerve ending sparked, then leaped to life when he kissed her forehead, her cheek and finally her lips.

He kept the kiss chaste, much to her disappointment. "Happy birthday, Brooke," he said with a tender smile.

"You know something? It is. Very happy."

He kissed her earnestly then. A kiss that promised passion. And untold secrets. A kiss that she wanted to last forever. But it didn't.

Jared pulled back and released a long whistle. "If we do that again, we might get arrested," he muttered, then shifted in his seat, his leg brushing against her thigh.

"But what a way to make headlines," Brooke said, amazed at how breathless she sounded. Amazed at how her feelings for him had robbed her of common sense.

He rested his hand on her knee underneath the cover of his jacket and drew lazy circles round and round much the same as he had on her arm. She'd never considered her knees an erogenous zone until Jared Granger's skilled touch.

Brooke had also never been so excited in her life. So pumped up in public. So tuned in to her own sexuality, her yearning to be daring. Something totally out of character for her.

A small sound bubbled up in her throat when his fingertip slipped just underneath her hem.

"What's wrong?" he asked.

"Nothing's wrong." At the moment everything was right.

He made passes up the inside of her knee, moving

ever so slightly upward to the inside of her thigh. Not an overt gesture by any means, but enough to make her want more. She almost lost it and yelled for him to keep going. She shuddered as if he touched intimate places now warm and damp, craving his attention.

She muffled another needy sound threatening to escape by resting her lips against Jared's neck.

"You're driving me crazy," he muttered.

She was driving *him* crazy?

He slipped his hand from underneath the jacket, but not before grazing her breast with a feather touch.

Brooke was practically panting. Practically ready to jump out of her skin, out of her clothes, and into his arms, not caring who played witness to her questionable behavior.

He had the nerve to check his watch. "It's almost eight. You'd better go."

Leaving his company wasn't something Brooke cared to consider at the moment. Not in her state of mind. Maybe she should reconsider exactly how she wanted to celebrate her birthday and with whom.

Brooke realized she was going to have to face her mother's wrath head-on if she canceled their dinner plans. But this particular chance was one she wanted to take. Needed to take. And it could very well be the only chance she would have.

"You're right," she said. "I better go. We better go. Back to my apartment before we do get arrested. Because if you don't take me away from here now, I won't be responsible for what I do to you here on this boat."

He looked totally taken aback by her declaration. "What about your family dinner?"

She ran her thumb along his jaw, suddenly aware of his clean-shaven face. He'd managed to do several things today, including turning her into a woman desperately in need of his full attention. A woman ready to take the ultimate gamble. "I can have dinner with them anytime."

His surprise turned to concern. "Brooke, I don't want to keep you from your family."

"Shh." She placed a fingertip to his lips to silence him. "Tonight I have other things in mind."

He grinned. "Oh, yeah. What other things?"

If she didn't want to kiss him so badly, she'd smack him. "Since you're determined to play dumb, guess I'll just have to show you."

He cupped her cheek in his palm. "Are you sure this is what you want?"

"I've never been so sure of anything in my life."

And she *was* sure—except for the fact that she was dangerously close to falling in love with Jared Granger in spite of her vow never to do something so inadvisable again.

Eight

The moment Brooke rushed through her apartment door, the phone started ringing. She had made record time driving to the complex. Obviously, she hadn't been quick enough to avoid a call from her mother before she had a chance to bow out gracefully. As far as she knew, Jared wasn't too far behind. Hopefully she could get off the phone before he arrived.

Taking in hand all the excuses she'd rehearsed on the way, she grabbed up the cordless phone. "Speak now or forever hold your peace." For some reason the greeting seemed appropriate. For some reason she felt silly.

"Brooke, is that you?"

Thank heavens it was her mother and not Macy calling about a schedule change. "Yes, Mom, it's me. I just got in."

"Late night at work?"

Should she lie? No. She didn't need to lie. Besides, whose life was it, anyway? Hers. "Actually, I met a friend for drinks." So far, so good. "It took longer than I expected."

"Then will you be over soon?"

Now for the nitty-gritty. "If you don't mind, I think I'll take a rain check on dinner."

"But, Brooke, dear, I made meat loaf."

Like that wasn't a common occurrence every Tuesday. "Yes, I know, but you, Dad and Michelle still have to eat, right?"

"Yes, that's true." Her mother's disappointment was palpable, even through the phone line.

Brooke tamped down the sudden guilt with an offer. "Tell you what. We can have breakfast together in the morning. My first appointment isn't until nine."

"Well, okay, dear. If you insist. Whatever makes you happy. After all, it is your birthday."

Exactly. "Thanks, Mom. Is Michelle there?"

"Of course."

Of course. Michelle, ever the loyal daughter. "Can I talk to her for a minute?"

"Yes, you may."

While waiting for Michelle to make her way to the phone, Brooke was startled by a sudden rap on the door. Her heart jumped, then started to pump at a furious rate. Her palm began to perspire where she gripped the phone. Unquestionably warm, she shed her jacket on the way to the door, tossed it on the sofa and laid the rose Jared had given her on the coffee table.

Opening the door, Brooke found Jared on her threshold, all sexy smile and untamed sensuality. She put her finger to her mouth, signaling him to be quiet, wishing she could kiss him into silence instead.

Once he entered and closed the door behind him, Brooke turned her back just in time to hear Michelle say, "Where in the heck are you? Do you realize I've had to endure Mom's grilling for over an hour now?"

Michelle's attitude didn't bode well for Brooke's impending request. "Did she go to a lot of trouble?"

"Just the usual Tuesday night fare. Oh, she did buy a frozen pound cake. I suggested chocolate for a change, but she wouldn't budge because of your allergies."

"I'm sorry I'm going to miss it." *Fibber.*

"You're not coming over?"

"No. I have company."

"Who?"

"Someone."

A moment of silence followed. "You mean someone as in *him?*"

Jared chose that moment to slip his arms around her waist from behind and bury his face in her neck. "Bingo," Brooke said with a slight gasp.

"He's really there, in the apartment?"

"Yes. Live and in person." And at the moment right behind me with his hand in a place Mother wouldn't approve.

"I only have two words to say about that."

Feeling liquid-boned, Brooke leaned back against Jared and watched while he fumbled with the buttons on her blouse. "What would that be?"

"Safe sex," Michelle declared in her rah-rah voice.

"I've got it covered," Jared whispered, obviously hearing Michelle's edict through the receiver.

"I said 'save socks,' Mom, in case she gets any for her birthday," Michelle called out. "You are getting some for your birthday, aren't you, Brookie?"

Brooke cringed over the thought that her mother had been eavesdropping. "Do you think she bought that?"

"Who cares? You shouldn't. After all, you're old enough to do as you please."

Brooke was starting to have trouble following the conversation. Heck, she was having trouble following anything at the moment except Jared's fingertip tracing a path over the top edge of her now-exposed lace bra.

"I need to go," Brooke said on a sigh.

Michelle chuckled. "I just bet you do."

"So can you do me a favor and find some excuse to stay with Mom and Dad tonight?"

"As a matter of fact, I suddenly feel a debilitating headache coming on. Literally. It will probably force me into bed immediately after dinner."

"You're the best, Shelly." She suspected Jared was, too.

Michelle sighed dramatically. "I know. I'm wonderful and obviously a glutton for punishment. Just one more piece of advice before I hang up."

Brooke wasn't sure she could handle any advice, not with Jared's palm sliding up her stocking-covered thigh, taking her skirt with him. "What's that?"

"It doesn't have to be forever."

With that, the line went dead, and the cogs in

Brooke's brain started turning. Could she really treat this as a casual affair? A one-time fling? Probably not.

Too late to turn back now. She would just have to take that out and examine it later. Much later. Right now she had an impatient man undressing her and an overwhelming desire to let him.

After tossing the phone aside to join her jacket, Brooke turned in Jared's arms. He slipped the silk blouse from her shoulders then reached around to release the button on the back of her skirt.

"This is totally unfair," Brooke said as she lifted her chin to give his lips better access to her throat. "You haven't even taken off your jacket."

He raised his head and grinned. "You've already seen me in my birthday suit. I want to see you in yours."

"You have a point."

"No kidding." He pressed his hips to hers.

She definitely got the point.

When he began to lower her zipper, she reached behind and stopped him. Before things progressed, Brooke felt the need to make a necessary revelation. By doing so, she would be taking a risk that he would change his mind about going any farther. But she wanted this next step in their relationship to begin with total honesty. Or at least where her past was concerned.

She braced her hands on either side of his head and lifted his face from where he had it buried in her cleavage.

"Jared, there's something I need to tell you."

He raised a brow. "You've changed your mind?"

"No, but you might change yours once I tell you this."

He fondled her breast through the lace and smiled. "Unless you admit your name's really Bradley, I don't think that's going to happen."

"No, that's definitely not it." She lowered her eyes and gathered her courage. "I haven't been with anyone."

"You're a virgin?" His tone was nothing less than shocked.

Her gaze snapped to his. "I hate that word. Makes me sound like a saint. I'm not even close."

He dropped his hand and took a step back. "I guess this is probably a good time to ask your age."

"Twenty-seven."

"Okay, there's no chance of a felony being committed here. So what's the real problem?"

"I just figured that you probably think there's something wrong with me—"

"Brooke, I don't—"

"But there's nothing wrong. I wanted to wait—"

"Come here." Taking her hand, he effectively squelched her sudden outburst and led her to the sofa. Disappointment filled Brooke as they sat in silence. He was about to reconsider, exactly what she had feared might happen. Maybe that was for the best.

Cupping her jaw with his palm, he said, "I think it's admirable that you've waited, but I want you to be certain about this. Really sure."

She placed her hand over his. "I am, Jared. I wouldn't be doing this with just anyone."

Now he looked worried. "What do you see happening between us?"

"I hope you're going to take me to bed and ravage me."

"I mean as far as the future is concerned."

A tough question, Brooke decided. "I don't want to worry about that right now. I only know I want to be with you tonight. Then we'll see what happens."

"Only tonight?"

Brooke tried to keep the mood light, refusing to consider anything beyond the present. "That depends on if you live up to your reputation, Doctor."

"And what reputation is that?"

She sat forward and turned to work his jacket off his broad shoulders. "The one that claims you're as good in bed as you are in surgery."

He leaned his head back against the sofa. "Man, you're putting a lot of pressure on me."

"Not yet." Feeling brave, Brooke slid one fingertip up the obvious ridge in his slacks and back down, at the same time sending a steady stream of pleasant chills up her spine.

He clasped her wrist and brought her palm to his lips. "Now you've done it."

"You mean that's all there is to it?" She chewed her bottom lip and tried to look serious. "Boy, I was expecting so much more."

The next thing she knew he was lifting her into his strong arms. She kicked off her high heels and they hit the floor with a thump. She laughed at the thought of being seduced out of her shoes. Laughed at the exhilarating feelings. Laughed because she had never felt such freedom. Such need.

"I guarantee there's a lot more," he whispered, his breath warm on her face.

"I'm relieved."

"Now where's your bedroom?"

Brooke pointed past the kitchen to the small hall. "In there." Her voice sounded high-pitched, nervous.

Once in her darkened bedroom, he slid her slowly down his body—where they touched became a flashpoint of fire. He bracketed her face in his large palms. "Are you afraid?"

"Some." A lot. Not afraid of him. Afraid of what she was feeling. What she was about to do.

He touched his lips to hers. "I'll make it right."

Brooke somehow knew he would.

He kissed her then, a slow sultry mating of lips, gentle and persuasive, until all her worries slipped away. So did her skirt as he slid the zipper down, allowing the barrier to fall to the floor into a fabric puddle at her feet.

Now she was dressed in nothing more than her bra, pantyhose and gooseflesh. With only the hall light to guide him, Jared took her by the hand and led her to the bed. She expected him to lay her down, but instead he seated her on the edge. She did not expect him to reach for the bedside lamp and flip it on. The room was now filled with a soft glow, illuminating everything, including her half-naked form.

Suddenly ill at ease over her state of undress, Brooke resisted the urge to hide her face in her hands.

"Is it necessary to have the lights on?" she asked.

"At the moment, yeah," he said. "I want to see what I'm doing. I want to see you."

Brooke began to tremble when he slipped the clasp on her bra. He kissed her softly and whispered,

"Easy, babe," as he removed the garment and tossed it aside.

This wasn't at all easy, she decided. Her shaking resulted not only from self-consciousness, but also from his passionate gaze—and her concern over making love with a man who might not have the capacity to ever love her back.

"You're really beautiful, did you know that?"

No, not really. She had always tried to maintain a positive body image, but self-criticism sometimes surfaced. Her breasts were merely adequate, her hips too full, her ankles too thick. She hadn't been blessed with Michelle's height or long waist. Right now none of that seemed to matter. Not when Jared looked at her as if she were a priceless work of art.

Standing, he gently pushed her onto her back and began to work the panty hose down her hips and legs, bending to plant whisper kisses in their wake.

Once she was completely exposed to his eyes, he straightened and smiled. "You're blushing."

This time she did cover her face with her hands. "What do you expect with you just standing there, staring at me?"

"I'm not complaining. You look great in pink. All over."

She peeked between her hands and saw him struggling with the buttons on his shirt, his fingers shaking, his left-handed effort agonizingly slow.

Without thought, she moved from the bed and stood before him, naked as the day she was born and not really caring. "Let me do this."

The hard planes of his face, the unyielding set of his jaw, revealed his frustration. "I should be able to do it myself. I *can* do it myself, it just takes too damned long. Especially at a time like this.''

''It's okay. I know you can, but I want to do it.''

She concentrated on each button and, once she was done, yanked the tails from his waistband and stood on tiptoe to work the shirt away.

He tipped her chin up, and she met his gaze. ''You take good care of me.''

She gave him a smile. ''I'm only just beginning.'' And hopefully she wouldn't disappoint him later when it mattered most. Hopefully there would be no regrets.

Once she had his shirt off, Brooke was thankful for the light that enabled her to see his chest in all its glory. Not that she hadn't seen it before. Yet each time she appreciated the finer details more, especially now that she could look her fill without worrying if he noticed. She ran her fingers through the triangular tuft of gold-brown hair in the middle of his sternum. She traced a path down the vee pointing to his navel and the narrow line of darker hair that disappeared into his waistband.

Jared's breath hitched when she impulsively streaked her tongue over his flat brown nipple. He bent and whispered in her ear, revealing what he intended to do to her in very descriptive language that almost rendered her speechless. Not an easy feat by any means.

Brooke smiled up at him and simply said, ''Promise?''

''You bet.''

Normally Brooke wasn't a gambler, but tonight she'd wager her paycheck that Jared Granger would make good on that promise and perhaps even fulfill a few promises he hadn't mentioned, not that she could imagine he'd forgotten anything. Except, perhaps, the one promise she wished for most—the promise of a future with him in it.

He fished in his pockets and tossed its contents onto the nightstand. Brooke caught a glimpse of his keys, his wallet, and three condoms.

Three condoms? *Oh, wow.*

"You can finish undressing me now," he said with a half smile.

After another sweep down his belly with curious fingers, she reached his fly, lowered his zipper as well as her eyes to watch. Thankfully she saw a flash of white. At least he wasn't "going native" tonight, allowing her more time to prepare. As if she could prepare.

He kicked off his shoes and stepped out of his slacks, then waited stock-still for her to continue.

Drawing a deep breath, Brooke slipped her thumbs underneath each side of the briefs' waistband and guided them past his hips.

Even after the briefs fell to the floor, freeing him, she couldn't tear her eyes away. She certainly didn't dare look at his face to see his reaction to her ogling his attributes. Last night she had only caught a glimpse. Now she was getting a first-rate view. And some view it was. No doubt about it, he was all man, marvelously aroused, virile with a capital *V*.

And she simply *had* to touch him. Experience all that power in her hands. She started by grazing his generous length with one short, painted fingernail, then she circled her fingers around him, causing him to take in a deep draw of air. She marveled at his strength, his size, the differing textures—and his sudden reaction to her experimentation. Every muscle in his abdomen clenched.

He grasped her wrist, his jaw as rigid as his body. "Any other time I wouldn't mind you doing that," he said in a voice low and thick with desire. "But I'm just barely hanging on here. It's been a while, and I want to do this right. Make this good for you."

Though she wanted to see exactly how much control she wielded over him, she couldn't possibly argue with his reasoning. Later she would take her time, satisfy her inquisitiveness.

He led her back to the bed and tossed the covers completely away, then followed her down to the mattress. Braced on one elbow, he laid his left hand on her breast, casually stroking her nipple back and forth as she stared up at him, barely able to focus. Barely able to breathe.

"Tonight, when we were on that boat," he began, "I could have touched you, and no one would've known. I almost did."

Brooke concentrated on his flame-blue eyes, trying to stay focused on what he was saying, not what he was doing, as his palm traveled slowly down the curve of her hip, pleasantly abrading her skin. "I really wanted you to touch me," she admitted on a broken breath.

"I know. I could tell." He moved his hand to below her navel. "There was just one problem." He slid his fingers through her sheltering curls and paused before reaching ground zero.

Brooke swallowed hard and tried not to squirm her encouragement. "It wasn't private enough?"

"Yes, and no." He skated his fingertip lower and homed in on exactly where she needed him to be, centering on the place that craved fulfillment. His touch began to appease the desperate, throbbing ache. She whimpered like a lost child, over the delicious sensations.

"That's the problem," he said, stroking her tenderly with tiny circles, stoking the fire. "It's those sounds you make."

"I'm sorry. I can't help it."

He slipped one finger deep inside her. She moaned again. "Don't apologize," he said. "I love it. But you would have given us away for sure."

Brooke thanked her lucky stars that her apartment was on the second floor and positioned in the corner, because right now she was on the verge of making a few sounds that might rouse the heaviest sleeper, or possibly her mother who happened to be five miles away.

Jared hovered over her, not missing a beat with his sensual caresses or his steady gaze. She balanced on the brink of something incredible, the pressure building and building beneath his proficient fingertips. The man was obviously becoming ambidextrous. He certainly had no problem utilizing his left hand in this endeavor. He made it seem effortless and heavenly.

Brooke drifted away into bliss on the wings of Jared's intoxicating cologne, carried off by the sensuality of his assessing blue eyes and the urgency of his fantastic fingers. With one more touch, she would be totally consumed by a release she wasn't sure she could endure quietly.

Then suddenly he was no longer touching her. She groaned at the loss.

"Just a minute," he said, his breathing almost as unsteady as hers. He rose up and reached over her to retrieve a condom. "Trust me, Brooke. It will be better this way."

She had no doubt he knew exactly what he was doing.

He sat up, tore open the package and rolled the condom on. He nudged her legs apart and straddled her thighs, then leaned forward to take one nipple in his mouth, commanding her body again with his fine fingertips as he suckled her breast. She raced quickly past the bounds of coherent thought as the climax overpowered her and sent her straight into glorious gratification. So overcome by the steady pulse of fulfillment, Brooke barely realized he was poised to enter her. And as he filled her with one long thrust, her body drew him inside of its own accord.

The pleasure mixed with pain. She cried out from both.

He was so still against her. So powerful in her arms. So gentle when he whispered, "I'm sorry, babe. Just hang on a minute."

Jared made the request as much for himself as for her. He needed to give her time to adapt and allow himself time to regain his bearings. Every muscle in his body went rigid as he fought to stay in control. Fought his body's demand for a much-needed release.

It had been way too long since he'd made love. Too long since he had really cared about a woman.

Had he ever really cared this intensely? Wanted someone as badly as he wanted Brooke? Not that he could recall.

He could do nothing more than surrender to her, the unfamiliar emotions welling inside him. Brooke was so tight surrounding him, so warm and wet and good. Probably too good for him. Too damned good to hold on much longer.

But he had to, for her.

He slipped his arms behind her back and buried his face in the sweet scent of her neck. Holding her did little to convince his body not to act from instinct, but it did a world of good for his soul. She had truly given him everything, and he probably didn't deserve it. She definitely deserved a considerate lover. That he could manage.

"Are you okay?" he whispered.

"If I were more okay, I'd probably suffer cardiac arrest."

He lifted his face to study her dark eyes. "Then I'm your man." There was an irony to those words. Would he ever be that to her? Did he want that kind of commitment? Was he ready to face all the feelings crowding in on him?

She moved beneath him impatiently, tossing away his concerns. He sank inside her a little more. "Do you have any idea how great you feel?" His voice came out in a gruff whisper from the effort it took to speak.

"Probably as great as you feel inside me." She sounded just as throaty with need.

He moved a little faster this time, drove a little deeper. "Am I hurting you?"

"No. Not now."

He felt her relax and took the cue to answer his own body's demand. He tried to temper his movements so he wouldn't cause her more pain, but then she wrapped her legs around his waist, and that was all it took. He set the rhythm nature and his body dictated and gave himself over to it without hesitation. She trembled beneath him, and he realized he was trembling, too. Damn near shaking with the force of his need.

"Brooke, Brooke..." he said on a ragged breath as he reached to touch her again and again with greedy hands. He couldn't seem to get enough of the feel of her.

She met him stroke for stroke, small sounds of pleasure slipping between her parted lips. She was close to release, and he clung to every last shred of his will, determined that she take this trip with him. And she did, right before he gave up and gave in.

The crest shook him to the core. Took him to a place he couldn't remember ever going. Brought on feelings he'd never before experienced.

He wrapped Brooke securely in his arms, content to simply hold her, something totally foreign to him. More times than he cared to admit, with other women, he had stayed only a few moments, avoiding any kind of real intimacy. Rarely did he spend the night with anyone, but he couldn't even consider leaving Brooke until morning. Maybe not even then.

He had known lovers who were much more experienced, much more wild in their demands, but he'd never known anyone so sweet as Brooke Lewis. Or anyone so good, inside and out.

After a time he slipped his arm from beneath her and sat up, trying to escape the emotions. Escape the urge to tell her exactly what he was feeling. Not until he could sort things out.

"Where are you going?" she asked.

"Nowhere. I'm trying to catch my breath."

He glanced at her face, soft with satisfaction. But in her eyes he saw concern.

When he stretched out beside her once again, she snuggled close to his side and proclaimed, "I'm starving. My stomach sounds like a freight train."

Jared chuckled. "So that's what I heard? And I thought you were just feeling really good."

She raised her head and sent him a pretend pout. "I can't believe with all your medical knowledge that you can't tell the difference between sexual rumblings and hunger pangs."

Laughing, he wrapped her in his arms again, relishing her body against his and the sudden lightness in his heart, surprised that he could feel so relaxed yet so ready to make love to her again. But he would wait for now. Give her time to recover. Give *himself* time to recover. In the meantime they could have something to eat. Considering what he had planned for the rest of the evening, they'd both need sustenance to maintain their strength.

He brushed a kiss across her forehead and pushed himself up on one elbow. "What do you have in the fridge?"

She studied the ceiling. "Not much. I have a bagel but no cream cheese. Some kind of whole-grain cereal. And I think I have a can of fruit salad."

"Interesting diet."

She smiled. "Sorry. I tend to eat out a lot."

"I guess I vote for the fruit, then."

She slipped out of bed, taking the top sheet to wrap herself in a full-body cocoon. Jared imagined unwinding that sheet when she returned. He imagined a lot of things. "Got any whipped cream for the fruit?"

Her hand poised on the door, she faced him again with a knowing smile. "No. Just some low-fat yogurt."

"No, thanks. Guess the fruit will have to do."

Bracing one shoulder against the door, she asked, "Are you considering utilizing that fruit in some very naughty ways, Dr. Granger?" She pushed her curls away from her face. "I certainly hope so."

"Why don't I just surprise you?"

She flashed him a fatal, dimpled grin, a combination of sultry sensuality and inviting innocence. "Good. I love surprises."

Normally Jared didn't like them at all, but Brooke Lewis—part seductress, part saint—was proving to be the best surprise of all.

Nine

Brooke slowly opened her eyes and immediately zeroed in on the bedside table littered with telltale signs of lovemaking. The scent of musky cologne and sweet nectar filtered into her senses, thrusting her into wakefulness. Shards of memories, keen as a pinprick, invaded her muddled thoughts.

Rolling over, she found only an empty space beside her, still warm from Jared's ever-present heat. Obviously, he hadn't been gone too long. She hated the fact that he hadn't wakened her to let her know he was leaving, but he had left behind the rose along with a business card resting on the adjacent pillow.

She picked up the card and found a handwritten note on the back. Not the neatest penmanship, but remarkably legible for a doctor:

"Thanks for the picnic. See you tonight for more therapy—Jared."

Brooke placed the paper to her lips and stroked the rose down her cheek, recalling Jared's touch, his ardent kiss, the way he had made love to her so thoroughly.

Setting both the rose and card aside, she sank back onto her pillow. She felt pleasantly sore all over. And sticky. The man had done things with canned fruit that went beyond all her imaginings. Beyond all her expectations.

She hadn't realized making love could be so much fun. So exhilarating. So intoxicating. But then again, she'd never even considered having a man like Jared Granger as her first lover. How very lucky for her. And he wanted to see her again tonight. At least it was a start.

Smiling at her good fortune, Brooke grudgingly checked the bedside clock—7 a.m. If she didn't force herself into the shower, she'd be late for work.

The doorbell sounded, sending Brooke from the bed in a rush. Excitement raced through her over the prospect that the very good doctor had returned.

She grabbed her robe from the end of the bed and slipped it on. On a whim she picked up the rose and placed it in her teeth, feeling as playful as she had the evening before. If luck prevailed, maybe he'd like to shower with her. Of course, then she would really be late. But what a wonderful excuse for tardiness. Not that she would actually use it.

When Brooke opened the door, her mouth dropped open. The rose hit the floor.

Jeanie Lewis stood on the threshold, not Jared Granger.

Her mother put on her no-nonsense face. "Good

heavens, Brooke, what are you doing with a flower in your mouth? Do you have any idea how unsanitary that is?''

Brooke was surprised that her mother hadn't warned her she might put her eye out with the stem. But then, Jeanie hadn't seen her wayward daughter running to the door. ''It was a joke, Mom. I thought you were Michelle.'' A convenient lie.

Without waiting for an invitation, Jeanie brushed past Brooke. ''Michelle's already at work.'' She held up a white pastry box. ''I stopped by the bakery down the street and brought some fresh whole-wheat bagels and strawberry preserves.''

Too bad Brooke hadn't had the preserves last night. She could think of several sensual possibilities, which immediately caused her face to fire up. ''Why are you here, Mom? And why didn't you use your key?''

''I left it in my other coat.'' Jeanie set the box aside and removed her jacket. She faced Brooke with disappointment calling out from her features. ''We're having breakfast for your birthday, remember?''

How had Brooke forgotten that? Of course, Jared had totally occupied her thoughts, as well as her time, for the past few hours, not her mother. ''Great. Let's eat. I'm running late.''

Jeanie surveyed Brooke up and down suspiciously. Could her mother actually see the effects of Jared's lovemaking? Were the changes obvious? Did she look that different? She certainly felt different.

''I realize you're far from being ready for work,'' Jeanie said, pulling back a chair from the dinette. ''So just have a seat and start eating. I'll be right back to join you just as soon as I strip your bed.''

Alarms rang out in Brooke's head as she followed her mother down the hall, resisting the urge to grab her up and carry her back into the kitchen, away from any damning evidence. "That's not necessary, Mother. I'll do it later."

"It's no trouble at all. I'll just take your sheets home with me and bring them—" Jeanie pulled up short immediately inside the bedroom door.

Brooke could just imagine the scene unfolding before her mother's eyes—the lone unopened condom sitting on the nightstand next to the two empty foil packets, Jared Granger's other legitimate calling card, an empty bowl, tangled sheets, Brooke's pantyhose and best skirt still lying on the floor.

With slow, stilted movements, Jeanie made her way to the nightstand and picked up the condom. She turned and held it up as if it were a dead cockroach. "What is this?"

"A condom."

"Would you care to explain what it's doing here?"

No, she wouldn't. "Would you believe I used them as party balloons?"

Jeanie's glance shot to the war zone sheets. "I certainly hope that's true, but I have a feeling it's not."

An opportunity had presented itself to Brooke, and she wasn't about to ignore it. Time for getting down and dirty with the truth. Time to lay all the cards on the table and let them fall where they may. Long past time.

Brooke grabbed the condom from her mother and tossed it back onto the table, then took her by the hand and led her to the dining room, away from the proof of one wonderful night of passion. She pulled out two chairs, face-to-face, and prepared to say the things she should have said years ago.

"Mom, in case you haven't noticed, I'm a woman now. That means I can do my own laundry, clean my own house, live my own life. I appreciate everything you've done for me, but I'm not that sickly little girl who lived her formative years dependent on you to make it all better."

Although her mother looked stunned, Brooke decided to continue while she still had the courage. "I'm also old enough to have a healthy relationship with a man, as hard as that is for you to believe."

Jeanie's eyes misted. "Do you love him?"

The question caught Brooke totally off guard. Did she love him? "I care a great deal for him." Deep down she knew it was more than simple caring, a scary concept, but something she couldn't deny.

"Is he married?"

"Absolutely not. He's a good man. He's going through a tough time right now, and I'm happy to say I'm helping him get through it."

Jeanie's face flashed anxiety like lights on the Las Vegas strip. "He doesn't have a job." It wasn't a question.

Brooke didn't bother to stifle her laughter. "Actually, at the moment he's on medical leave, but he's not a bum. He's a doctor."

Now her mother looked hopeful. "A pulmonary specialist?"

"A cardiac surgeon. The best. Only he's had an injury to his hand. I've been his therapist the past few weeks."

"Is that legal, having…" Her mother's gaze slid

away. "I mean, having relations with a patient, is that wise?"

A few weeks ago Brooke would have said no. So much had changed. *She* had changed. "I'm no longer his official therapist, so it's okay."

Jeanie regarded Brooke with eyes brimming with unshed tears. "I'm sorry, honey. I just worry about you. I don't want you to get hurt."

Brooke clasped her mother's hands between her palms. "You can't protect me from everything, Mom. Michelle, either. You've raised two sensible girls." For the most part. "You should be proud."

"But what about Brandon? Don't you remember how he devastated you?"

Brooke mentally cringed. Why was everyone so bent on beating the past to a pulp? "He's been out of my life for more than six years. And to tell the truth, our relationship never evolved past late-night studying and an occasional kiss. I was young and, yes, somewhat naive. I never really loved him. I only thought I did." A revelation that had hit home last night in Jared Granger's arms.

Jeanie swiped at her damp eyes. "Brooke, I walked the floors with you night after night when you were little and your asthma got the best of you. All those times when you couldn't catch your breath and your face was blue and I was so afraid I'd lose you, I tried to protect you as best I could. But I can't protect you against getting hurt by a man. I wish I could."

"You don't have to worry about that, Mom. I don't expect you to shelter me from everything. I have to learn those lessons on my own. And I do know what you went through with my asthma. I couldn't have gotten through it without you and Dad.''

''I just hope you know what you're doing now, but I don't see what this *man* has to do with me washing your clothes. Taking care of the little things.''

''It has to do with independence. My need to make it on my own. Can you please try to understand that?''

''I suppose so.'' Her tone was less than agreeable. ''Does this man have a name?''

''Jared.''

Jeanie's eyes widened. ''Shelly's boyfriend?''

For a moment Brooke was confused until she recalled the night she'd told her mom that very thing to avoid an explanation. ''No, Mom. He's not Shelly's boyfriend.''

Brooke drew her mother into a heartfelt hug and patted her back. ''It will be okay, Mom. I'm always going to be your little girl. And I love you.''

''I love you, too, dear heart.'' Jeanie pulled away and sent Brooke a tentative smile. ''Just promise me one thing.''

Oh, boy. ''What's that?''

''Don't tell your father about this. He's still having trouble with the fact you're old enough to wear a bra.''

They shared a laugh and another hug. Brooke felt exceedingly buoyed by the conversation. Liberated. And she had Jared Granger to thank for the sudden sense of freedom. She planned to tell him that—and more—tonight. After she talked with his doctor.

''Dr. Kempner will see you now, Ms. Lewis.''

Brooke followed the nurse down the hallway to the

doctor's private office. Glancing at her watch, she realized she didn't have much time left before her next appointment. But she didn't want to discuss Jared's problem over the phone or the fact she was no longer his official therapist. How she would handle that remained to be seen.

Nick Kempner stood when Brooke entered. "Hey, Brooke."

Brooke took the hand he offered for a friendly handshake then sat across from him. "Sorry to interrupt your schedule on such short notice, but I'll make this quick."

"No problem." Dr. Kempner pulled his chair back and settled in. "I assume you're here to discuss Dr. Granger."

"Yes. I thought you needed to be aware of a few things."

"Okay. What's up?"

Brooke folded the hem of her lab coat back and forth. "His hand is doing much better. He can almost make a fist, except for his second digit."

"Still rigid?"

"Yes. It's not responding to the treatment like I'd hoped. I think he's developed a contracture."

Dr. Kempner sat back in his chair and sighed. "Have you mentioned this to him?"

She tried to keep the guilt from her face. "I warned him what could happen at first. Recently I told him to give it more time, but I think his time's up."

"Which means he's probably going to have to have a tendon release." Dr. Kempner tossed a chart aside. "Damn. I wanted to avoid that. Normally I'd wait at least six months to even consider the surgery, but knowing Jared, he'll push for it just to get it over with."

"Jared's—" Boy, she had really done it now. "Dr. Granger's been doing so well. His attitude's good and he's been working hard. I'm worried this is going to set him back."

"It will. But with your help, he'll get through it."

Confession time. "Actually, he dismissed me as his therapist."

"I know."

Brooke's chest contracted, forcing the oxygen from her lungs. "You do?"

"Yeah. Your boss contacted me."

She had no idea what Macy had said, or if she should even ask. "I see."

Kempner leaned forward and studied her with an unwavering gaze. "What's going on between you and Jared, Brooke?"

Brooke considered dancing around the truth but she assumed he would see right through her. "We've grown very close." *We're friends. Lovers.*

"So I assume you're still administering therapy privately. At least on some level."

She looked up to meet Dr. Kempner's grin. Now her face probably resembled a second-degree sunburn. "We haven't discussed what he's going to do about his therapy. This only happened two days ago."

His expression went serious. "I'm not here to judge you, Brooke. Things happen. Jared can be a tough character to deal with, but obviously you've managed to break through his iron will. You have my congratulations."

"I appreciate that."

"But I'm also going to warn you that when he does hear this news, he could very well withdraw again."

"I know. That's why I've put off telling him."

"That's why you need to let me handle it."

Yes, that would be the professional thing to do, but would that be fair to Jared? Would he eventually resent her for not being honest? "Maybe it would be better coming from me."

"I have to make the diagnosis, Brooke. All you can do is tell him your suspicions, and I prefer you not do that in case you're wrong."

Oh, that she were wrong. "I've seen this before. Many times. I'm almost positive—"

"Let me be the bad guy."

Brooke would feel like the bad guy if she continued to keep her suspicions from Jared. Yet Dr. Kempner proposed to take the responsibility out of her hands. That was the professional avenue. Her personal relationship with Jared had muddied the boundaries. Yet she realized she had little say in the matter, at least where his doctor was concerned. Dr. Kempner was right. She could be wrong about the diagnosis. She needed to remain objective. Much easier said than done.

She sighed. "When do you plan on telling him?"

"He has an appointment with me tomorrow morning. I'll lower the boom then."

Brooke would see Jared tonight. How could she continue to act normal when so much was at stake for him? For her.

All the years of training had not prepared her for this situation. If she hadn't let herself get involved against her better judgment, if she'd remained emotionally detached, then she wouldn't be presented with this dilemma.

But she was emotionally involved, and Nick Kempner was probably right. He was Jared's doctor and the news should come from him. Then why did she feel like Judas?

"Okay," she said as she stood. "You should tell him."

Nick joined her at the door. "One more thing."

"What?"

He studied her with genuine concern. "Take care of him, Brooke. He'll need you more now than he's ever needed anything, even his career."

Brooke realized in that moment that she needed Jared, too. Needed him in her life. Needed his love. She prayed for the courage to tell him tonight. After tomorrow she might never get that chance again.

"Can you try a little harder?"

"It's too stiff."

"I know, but you're not concentrating."

"Yes, I am." That wasn't exactly the truth. Jared was concentrating all right—on Brooke's sexy lips that formed a straight line of disapproval, her great body hidden by jeans and a knit shirt, her midnight eyes regarding him with concern—not the annoying ball in his palm.

When he'd invited Brooke to his home in the city, he hadn't expected her to show up with her little bag of tricks intent on putting his hand through more therapy. But she'd insisted they have a session even though she wasn't officially his therapist any longer.

She was officially his lover, and that's all he could think about at the moment. That and the fact he had so much he wanted to say to her, if only he could find the courage.

Instead, he asked, "Aren't we done yet?"

She yanked the ball from his hand and tossed it into the bag a few feet away, making a perfect three-pointer into the goal. "I guess we are since your mind's somewhere else."

He couldn't argue that. And he couldn't get a grip on her attitude tonight. Quite different from last night when her laughter had come easily. When she'd been all willing woman in his arms. Tonight she had barely kissed him, just a quick peck at the door. He intended to get to the bottom of her mood.

Leaning across the table, he took her hand into his. "What's wrong, Brooke?"

She looked away. "Nothing. I'm just wondering if there's something I should have done to make your finger work better."

"You've done a great job. Like you said, it just takes time."

She brought her gaze back to his, apprehension in her eyes. "I guess you're right."

He intended to get her mind off his hand and onto more interesting subjects. "Do you want the nickel tour of the house now?"

Finally a smile. "Sure. Might as well get started, considering its size." They both stood at the same time. Again he took her hand, quickly guiding her past the kitchen and through the den, intentionally heading toward the bedroom. He planned to order takeout, right after he had his fill of Brooke as an appetizer.

Before he reached the hall leading to his bedroom, Brooke halted at the weight room. "Well now, this explains it," she said, strolling to the weight bench. "No wonder you're in such great shape."

"Was. Haven't been doing any lifting in a while."

She stretched out on her back on the narrow black table then pushed up the sleeves on her blouse, the barbells now positioned above her chest. She ran her fingers over them with an almost erotic caress. "Hmm. Wonder if I could bench press this."

Jared stood at the door, admiring the view of Brooke laid out on the table like a banquet, imagining her hands on him instead of the weights. "Don't even try it."

She lifted her head. "You don't think I can do it, do you?"

"Oh, I think you can, but I'm not sure what kind of shape you'll be in afterward. But if you're determined, go ahead. I know a good neuro guy when you hurt your neck."

She laughed, filling Jared with relief that her mood had lightened.

Brooke inched down the table from beneath the weights and crooked a finger at him. "Come here, big guy."

She didn't have to ask him twice. He was on his knees beside her in a matter of seconds. She grasped his neck and brought his mouth to hers, kissing him urgently. She nipped at his lips, stroked his tongue with her own, over and over until she had him completely under her control. Right now she could do anything to him and he wouldn't have the strength to put up a fight. Not that he really wanted to fight her.

By the time she broke the kiss, they were both winded.

"I've thought about this all day," she said. "About last night. I was in a total fog during my appointments."

He laid a hand on her bent knee. "I've had the strongest craving for fruit all day."

"That reminds me. Do you have any mangos available?"

He chuckled. "I don't think they're in season."

"Too bad."

"I plan on ordering Chinese. You should see what I do with those noodles." He lifted her top and planted kisses in the valley of her breasts above her bra.

"I can't wait."

Neither could he. He raised his head and met her sultry dark gaze. "Do you want me to call it in now?"

"Not yet." She looked around the room before bringing her attention back to him. "Right now I'm in the mood for a workout."

Not exactly the kind of exercise he'd envisioned. "Help yourself to the equipment."

She stroked his thigh. "I intend to."

The tightening in his groin indicated his willingness to let her. "You're bad, Brooke Lewis."

"You make me that way."

"I like you that way."

She grinned. "So what are we waiting for?"

"Not a thing. Follow me."

He started to stand but she stopped him by gripping his arm. "What's wrong with here?"

"You mean make love in a weight room?"

"Why not?"

"Because I generally don't keep condoms in here."

She sat up and pulled her top up over her head and dropped it on the floor. "Why don't we start here then just work our way to the bed? It could be part of the tour." She released the bra and tossed it onto the nearby treadmill with a sassy grin.

Jared could only stare at her round breasts and rosy pink nipples, amazed and thrilled by her total lack of inhibition. He pushed her back onto the table and took one peak into his mouth while undoing the fly on her jeans. She helped him slip the denim away, leaving her dressed in only a scrap of black satin. Working his way down with kisses, he paused at her belly and looked up to find her watching him, her expression mellowed by desire.

"Speaking of workouts," he said, "are you sore?"

"I was surprised I could walk normally today. Not that I'm complaining, mind you."

"Maybe I can make it better."

He grasped her ankles and gently pulled her down until her bottom rested at the end of the table and her feet on the carpeted floor, giving him better access. He slipped off her loafers and socks then planted kisses on her delicate ankles, her well-shaped calves, nudging her knees apart to make his way slowly upward to a prime destination.

"Oh, my," she whispered, causing Jared to smile. He placed a kiss through the satin. "How's that?"

"Keep going, Doctor. You're doing fine."

After working her panties away, he teased his tongue back and forth in the crease of her thigh. She made an impatient sound. Wanting to maintain the suspense, to keep anticipation high, Jared continued to feather more caresses with his lips, his tongue, but not quite reaching his goal.

"Your about to do me in," she murmured.

"That's my plan."

"It's working."

She wriggled beneath his mouth, letting him know she was more than ready for action. So was he.

Fireworks went off behind Brooke's closed lids when Jared finally found her sensitive center with his masterful mouth. She gripped the sides of the table, afraid that if she didn't she might actually slide away. Heat gathered low beneath his mouth like an impending electrical storm. This intimate kiss was almost more than she could stand without screaming. Never in her life had she felt so incredible, so in tune with every nerve ending. The exhilarating feelings Jared generated with a simple stroke of his tongue sent her spiraling into some unknown place she hadn't known existed until him.

She gave everything over to the sensations, only aware of this remarkable journey toward sweet bliss. She wanted to hold back the tide but couldn't. She didn't have that much strength of will. Not with Jared Granger as her guide.

The release hit her with the force of a gale, stealing her breath, spurring her heart rate, launching her into welcome mindlessness. Her body quaked uncontrollably. The next thing she knew Jared was pulling her into his arms, holding her fast against his chest, his strong heart beating against her cheek.

"Wow." It was all she could think to say.

He rested his lips against her forehead. "How was that for a workout?"

"The most fun I've ever had in a gym." She suddenly realized he was still fully dressed in his jeans and T-shirt, and she was totally in the buff.

She smiled up at him. "I can't believe this happened again. I'm naked, and you have on all your clothes."

"We can remedy that shortly. But first, the bedroom."

He pulled her up, then, and taking her by surprise, tossed her over one shoulder like a sack of feed. "Oh, my gosh, you are a caveman," she said, laughing all the way down the hall.

"You bring out the Neanderthal in me," he said with an added pat on her bare butt.

Once in the dimly lit room, he laid her out on the bed with a gentleness that belied his earlier strength. He studied her face for a long moment before speaking. "I don't remember ever enjoying pleasing someone as much as I enjoy pleasing you," he said in an all-too-serious voice.

"And you do please me. So much."

He placed a tender kiss on her lips, no more than a whisper, but it made her want more. "You know something, I've never really enjoyed lovemaking before. Not like this."

"Really? Why not?"

"It's always been just a physical release. I've never

talked to a woman before, and I sure as hell never laughed before.''

She raked her fingers through his thick, golden hair. ''I can't imagine not talking or laughing if it feels right. Making that connection seems important.''

''It never was. Until now.''

Brooke's heart soared on a current of emotion. She was close to believing in the possibility of love once again, hopeful that he might care as much for her as she did for him.

He stood and undressed while she watched, his beautifully sculpted body finally bare to her eyes, along with an emotion in his expression she couldn't quite peg. She saw desire there, and maybe something more. Or perhaps she wanted to see it so badly that she was simply imagining things.

He came back to her with more gentle touches and kisses. He filled her body with fluid strokes and rocked her world with his power. Everything centered on this moment, the way he made her feel—totally and completely loved. She held on to him so tightly, afraid she might open her eyes and he would be gone. That this union—both physical and emotional—was only a dream.

But he was real. So real. Strong and alive. And deeply enfolded in her heart as well as her arms.

When he shuddered and called her name in a gruff whisper, it seemed natural to finally tell him. To take the ultimate chance. Whatever happened from this point forward would be in his healing hands.

''I love you, Jared.''

Ten

―――

Hearing Brooke say the words was like frigid water in Jared's face. He stilled, waiting for the overwhelming need to get out while he still could, as he had done several times before with other women. It didn't come.

Instead, a strong sense of well-being settled on his heart. He didn't feel threatened. He didn't want to head for the door. He needed to tell her something, although he wasn't sure what. Did he love her? Probably so. Or as close as he had ever come.

He rolled to his side and held her, but couldn't quite get a grasp on what he wanted to say.

She touched his face. "Don't look so scared, Dr. Granger. You don't have to say anything; I just wanted you to know."

"I'm not real good at this kind of thing."

"I would have to argue that."

He looked down on her and smiled. "I meant the commitment part."

"Did I ask for a commitment?"

"No. But you deserve one." He slipped his arms from around her and sat up with his elbows resting on bent knees. A few moments of silence passed before he asked, "How do you know for sure?"

She moved behind him and came to her knees, placing her hands on his shoulders. "Because unless I was in love, I would never give my heart to someone that I could very well lose."

He regarded her over one shoulder. "Who says you're going to lose me?"

"Let's just say I've had some experience with this."

He lowered his head and sighed. "Then you've lost someone you loved."

"Hasn't everyone loved and been left before?"

"No. Not me." He'd always been the one to do the leaving.

"Problem is, sometimes need gets tangled up with emotions," she said. "Need isn't enough to sustain a serious relationship."

The concern in her tone turned him around on the bed to face her. "What does that have to do with us?"

"It has to do with my first real relationship. He needed me to help him through school. I needed his companionship, his love. But once he reached his goal, I was no longer in the picture."

No wonder she had been so worried about his own motives, Jared thought. She had no cause for concern.

"So you're telling me that you still believe this relationship has only to do with me needing you."

"Does it?"

He streaked both hands down his face. "Brooke, I'd be lying if I said I didn't need you, but it goes beyond the therapy. If not for you, I would've given up on my career. Now I finally believe I'll be going back to surgery again, and a lot sooner than I expected."

She looked away. "Everything you've just said has to do with the therapy, not how you feel about me. Me, as a woman, not as your therapist."

He cupped her cheek and forced her attention back to him. "I care a lot about you, Brooke. I admire your guts and the way you make me laugh even when I'd rather punch the wall. You make love to me like no one I've ever known before, and I think about you every minute of every day when we're not together. Does that help?"

She draped her arms around his neck. "That's a start. So why don't we just take it one day at a time and see what happens from here on out?" Her tone lacked enthusiasm.

He would just have to show her that he wasn't at all like the man who'd obviously wrecked her heart. "Sounds like a plan to me." He kissed her once again, stirring his body and his soul. After breaking the kiss, he asked, "Are you hungry?"

She pushed him onto his back and sent him a wicked smile. "Oh, yeah."

As Brooke leaned over to kiss her way down his body, Jared decided he couldn't imagine spending his days without her. He had never known a woman completely willing to take a chance on him—a man who was as unqualified to judge matters of the heart as he was competent to perform delicate surgery. And one day soon he would be totally honest with her: he did love her, and damn if it didn't feel great.

"You owe me an explanation, Brooke."

Brooke froze in preparation for her next patient at the sound of Jared's voice. Two of her colleagues looked up from their own patients, more than mildly curious over the interruption and then pretended to go back to their business.

She slowly turned toward the treatment room door to find him standing there, arms folded across his chest, defiance in his eyes. The same defiance she had seen the first time he'd come to her as a patient, before everything had been complicated by emotions.

Brooke had spent most of the morning watching the clock, knowing that Jared's appointment with Dr. Kempner would be over soon, trying to prepare for the moment when she would have to face his questions head-on. The time had come sooner than she'd liked, and before she'd had ample time to prepare.

She took a few tentative steps forward. "Dr. Granger, if you'll just follow me to the—"

"Why the hell didn't you tell me?"

Without responding, she brushed past him in hopes that he would follow her. At least in the break room they might have some privacy, although there were no guarantees. But anything was better than engaging in a heated discussion with nosy onlookers present.

Once inside the break room, she found the receptionist sipping coffee and reading the paper. "Mary, could you give us some privacy?"

The young woman looked up at Brooke then centered her gaze on Jared, who stood stiff as a starched shirt, anger calling out from his blue eyes.

"Sure." Mary abandoned her coffee and rushed out of the room as if being chased by all the demons from hell.

Brooke slowly closed the door and faced Jared's wrath with minimal confidence. "I assume you've had your appointment with Dr. Kempner."

Jared walked to the window and kept his back to her. "You know that's exactly what I'm talking about." He turned to her once again, no less angry. "How could you keep something so important from me?"

"I had no choice."

"You had no right."

Brooke moved forward on jelly legs and braced her hand on the back of one plastic chair for support. "Dr. Kempner convinced me that it was the professional thing to do, and he was right. I'm not qualified to make that diagnosis."

Jared released a joyless laugh. "Professional? Lady, we went way beyond that. You should have told me. You, not Kempner. You owed me that much."

Did she owe him? Probably. But what was done was done, and she couldn't take it back. "Look, I only did what I thought was best. Besides, I didn't know for sure. Dr. Kempner said—"

"I don't give a damn about what Nick said!"

"Could you please keep your voice down?"

"Why? Are you afraid of losing your job? Well, join the crowd, because it looks like I've lost mine."

"That's not true. If you have the surgery—"

"I don't want to talk about the surgery." He moved toward her with a predatory gait. "I want to talk about honesty. Has everything you've told me been a lie?"

"No, of course not."

"And you expect me to believe that?"

She didn't know what she expected from him. She only knew she hated what she'd done and would probably live to regret it. "I know you're angry at me because I didn't tell you my concerns, but you have to understand that from the beginning I've worried about this happening. You were the one who blurred the lines. You were the one who insisted we could become involved without suffering any consequences, and I was a fool to let it happen."

"I guess I was a fool, too, wasn't I?"

Brooke's heart sat like a rock in her chest. She had no idea what to do, what to say, to convince him how very much she was hurting for him. How very much she needed to make it right. How very much she loved him.

"What do you want me to say?" she asked, trying hard to keep the tears from her voice, but to no avail.

The ire in his expression melted into defeat. "It's too late for you to say anything. You should've thought about that last night when you were in my bed, claiming you love me."

"I do love you."

"Do you? If you find it acceptable to lie to someone you supposedly care about, then I want no part of it.''

''I didn't exactly lie.''

He nailed her with a heart-wrenching glare. ''God, Brooke, let's not get into semantics here. You knew something was wrong, and you didn't tell me. Maybe that's a lie by omission, but it's still a lie.''

When he started past her toward the door, she grabbed his arm to stop him. ''Jared, please, don't leave until we talk about this some more.''

He shook off her hand. ''I'm tired, Brooke. Tired of talking. Tired of dealing with the uncertainty. I need to get away from here.''

He might as well have said he needed to get away from her. ''What about us?''

''Us?'' He thrust his hands into his pockets. ''I don't need any more problems, Brooke. I don't need anyone.''

All the frustration, the devastating emotions, tumbled down on Brooke in that instant like an avalanche. Anger took over. ''You are so wrong, *Dr.* Granger. You may not need me, but you need someone, unless you really buy into that old cliché of Physician, Heal Thyself. But if you want to go and bury yourself in self-pity, then be my guest. If you want to give up, then go ahead. I won't stop you this time.''

She drew in a ragged breath, her lungs burning, her heart aching. ''And someday I hope you realize that everything you are and can be goes far beyond being a doctor. No one realizes that better than me.''

Without a word he left the room with head lowered and shoulders slumped like a replay of their first encounter. Only this time he took pieces of Brooke's shattered heart with him.

Jared stared at the hospital room ceiling, his bandaged hand limp against his chest right above his wounded heart. He was several hours post-op and two weeks post-Brooke. The pain of surgery was nothing compared to the pain he had caused her and in turn had caused himself.

When the door clicked open, he turned his head expectantly, hoping against all hope it was her.

Instead, Nick Kempner strolled into the room and pulled up a chair. "How's my least favorite patient faring?"

Jared turned his face away from Nick's scrutiny. "I want to know when the hell I get out of here."

"Tomorrow morning."

"Great. The sooner, the better."

"She came by today. At noon."

Jared's gaze snapped back to Nick. "Who?"

Nick leaned his head back against the chair and released an impatient sigh. "Hell, Granger, don't play stupid with me." He pinned Jared with a stern look. "You know damn well I meant Brooke. She wanted to see how the surgery went, although I'm not sure why she bothered."

Neither did Jared, considering their last conversation. "Why the hell didn't she come in?"

"Why don't you tell me?"

Because he had treated her like dirt two weeks ago. Because he had too much stubborn pride for his own damn good, and it was killing him not to see her.

"Let's just say we had a heavy-duty disagreement over her not telling me about the contracture."

"That was my fault, not hers."

"She didn't have to listen to you."

"Yeah, as a matter of fact, she did." Nick pulled the chair closer to the bed and slumped back down with his legs stretched out, as if he planned to stay awhile. Jared wanted him to leave, before he had to answer more questions. Not likely that was going to happen.

"You put her in a precarious position, Granger. You know as well as I do that she was torn between doing her job and doing what was best for you. So if you're going to stay mad at the world, then start with me. Brooke doesn't deserve your anger."

Deep down Jared realized that now, but he didn't have a clue how to deal with it. "She doesn't deserve my problems. My career is in the toilet, and I suck at relationships."

"Don't we all, but that doesn't mean some things aren't worth chancing."

Jared leveled a frown on Nick. "That coming from a man who claims he's sworn off women."

"No. That's coming from a man who would give his right arm for the love of a good woman like Brooke."

"You don't even know her."

"But you do, and I can tell by your whipped-dog look the minute I mentioned her name that you have it bad for her. And she's got it pretty bad for you, too, although both of you are too obstinate to admit it."

Jared reached for the controls and raised the head

of the bed. If he could, he'd walk out of the hospital right now and go after her. "Okay, Kempner, you're right. I have it bad for her. Real bad. I just don't know what in the hell I should do about it. I was pretty rough on her the last time we spoke."

Nick rose from the chair. "Well, my man, I'm going to leave that up to you. I have no doubt you'll think of something. While I've got you captive in that bed, you might want to use your time coming up with some sort of plan. Diamonds work well."

"One more thing," Jared asked.

"Shoot."

"I have to speak at the pediatric fund-raiser in two days. Do you see any problem with that?"

Nick grinned. "Nope. I didn't operate on your mouth."

"Get out of here, Kempner."

"No problem. I've got three cases this afternoon waiting for me. And in a few months I expect you to be hounding me about delaying your next bypass."

"Don't I wish."

"No time to wish, Granger. Get with the program. You convinced me to go ahead and do the tendon release. It's all up to you now. You need to get back into the therapy program and work like hell. And like I told you from the beginning, the place to start is with Brooke. After all, she's the best therapist around. But I guess you know that by now."

Yeah, Jared knew that all too well. He also knew that he had lied, too. He needed her now more than ever. He loved her with an all-consuming passion that went far beyond anything he could ever comprehend.

Now if he could just convince her of that fact. Or was it too late?

Maybe not. He had two days before he returned to the hospital for the luncheon. Two days before he had the opportunity to see her again, if she came to the fund-raiser. He made a mental note to contact Michelle Lewis and make sure Brooke showed up. What he did after that point still remained to be seen. He'd just have to rely on his powers of persuasion—and hope they worked this time on Brooke.

Eleven

Thankfully Brooke wasn't too late for the luncheon, although she had no idea how she'd allowed Michelle to rope her into attending. She felt like a trout out of water among the medical crowd, but she would persevere, considering the event was for a good cause. The soon-to-be revamped pediatric unit needed all the supporters it could get, although Brooke had little to offer financially. At least she was able to make an appearance at the fund-raiser as her sister's guest.

Brooke milled around the hospital's banquet room, nibbling on the buffet offerings while watching Michelle in action. Her sister was the public relations queen-for-a-day, joking with several of the docs, shaking hands with the wives and generally having a field day doing her thing.

After a time Brooke took a seat at one round table

occupied by an older couple she didn't recognize. She started to introduce herself when Michelle appeared at the dais among the hospital administrators and chiefs of staff.

Michelle tapped the microphone to garner everyone's attention before speaking. "Ladies and gentleman, I want to thank you all for coming today. You are a great crowd, and we're thrilled that you're all as excited as we are here at Memorial about the new unit. And today we have a special guest who will hopefully encourage you to dig deep in those proverbial pockets."

A splattering of applause suspended Michelle's speech for a moment. She suddenly sent Brooke a quick glance that said, Here comes the good part.

Brooke toyed with a chocolate-dipped strawberry and glanced around the room, thinking it was too late to make a quick departure before the speaker commenced. Oh, well. Her next appointment wasn't until three so she would force herself to be attentive, or at least try.

Most days she hadn't been able to think about anything but Jared. Most nights, either. Two weeks had passed without a word from him, but that distance hadn't driven him from her mind or her heart. Two days ago she'd gone to see him after his surgery but chickened out. At least Nick Kempner had assured her that Jared had come through fine. The rest was up to him. He would require more months of therapy after the tendon release. Hopefully whomever Jared chose to administer that therapy would treat him right. If only he would choose her.

Many a moment she'd spent wallowing in her own

sorrow, wondering if she could have done anything differently. Wondering if she should try one more time to change his mind.

No, Jared would have to come to her. And the chance of that happening was equal to the chance that the guest speaker would turn out to be Harrison Ford.

"...please welcome Dr. Jared Granger."

Brooke's gaze shot to the front of the room. Surely she hadn't heard right. Surely she was dreaming. Of course she was. Michelle wouldn't intentionally drag her to this social soiree knowing she would be subjected to Jared's presence. That would be too cruel to fathom, and very unlike her sister.

But reality took hold as Jared made his way to the podium. Brooke dropped the strawberry to her plate.

The scene was so surreal, so unexpected, that Brooke's whole being went numb. He looked much the same as when she'd known him only as the elusive doctor. His hair was neatly combed, his suit impeccable, his right hand bandaged and splinted like before. The expression he wore was all business, confident. But in his eyes she saw a hint of vulnerability that as his friend she'd come to know. As his lover. And just seeing him again hurtled her heart into unwelcome sadness and loss.

She swallowed past the boulder in her throat and dug her nails into her palms to stop the threatening tears. She refused to cry in front of all these people. She refused to cry in front of him again.

Jared cleared his throat and looked out over the crowd, now silent and awaiting his words of wisdom. Brooke looked for a way out without being too obvious.

"I'm honored that Michelle Lewis asked me to be here today," he began. "I'm hoping it's because of my oratory skills and not due to the fact I was the only one without the schedule from hell."

While the patrons chuckled, Brooke clenched her jaw and stifled an oath.

Michelle? Michelle had asked him to deliver the luncheon address? Brooke wondered what the penalty would be for chaining a sibling in a closet for an interminable time. Might be worth it, considering the mean trick she'd just pulled.

Jared gripped the edge of the podium with his left hand and rested his bandaged one in front of him. His voice rang out clear as spring water over the now-silent crowd. "I'm glad you are all here today. By your presence, I believe you understand the need for this new unit. The need to make things better for our youngest patients, our greatest resource. And I—"

He paused for a long, painful moment, staring at the paper before him. He suddenly picked up that paper and crumpled it in his left hand then tossed it aside. "Right now I'm going to just say what's in my heart, so bear with me."

Among the spattering of whispers, Jared continued his impromptu speech. "A couple of months ago I lost a very special patient. She was a great kid, always optimistic despite the fact she spent several years on death's door. I couldn't save her, but she told me right before she died that she didn't blame me. Problem was, I blamed myself. You'd think a man would learn something from someone like that. But I didn't. Not until recently, when I had the opportunity to be a patient in this hospital."

Jared turned his gaze on Brooke, seeking, searching, but for what she wasn't sure. She wanted so badly to look away. Seeing him again was more agonizing than she'd ever envisioned. But she couldn't look away, even if her emotional survival depended on it. Right now she wanted to escape. Run for the nearest exit. Yet her body seemed glued to the chair by Jared's magnetic eyes and words.

"And I guess you could say I never realized how devoted the staff is here at Memorial until I had my accident," he continued. "I couldn't have made it the past few months without that staff, one person in particular."

Brooke felt as though everyone in the room had disappeared and that he spoke only to her. She felt as though she were trapped in a vacuum, battling hope that he was addressing only her, that she was the one who had made the difference in his life. Could she really believe that, or did she simply want it to be true?

"Everyone deserves a chance, especially children," he said. "Some people even deserve a second one. Life is too short to neglect those things that make our life complete." He inhaled and exhaled slowly. "Before this accident I didn't know how important it is to be surrounded by people you care about. I didn't know who I was beyond being a doctor. Now I know because of one very special woman."

He paused for a moment, his eyes locked on Brooke's. Tears drifted down her cheeks and she futilely tried to swipe them away.

Finally Jared took his gaze from Brooke and brought it back to the curious crowd. "So I hope be-

fore you leave here today, you'll get out those check-
books and give generously so that we can see this
pediatric unit become the best in San Antonio and
maybe even the state. That's really all I have to say,
so you can get back to your meal. Right now I have
something important I need to say to someone.'' He
sighed and lowered his head before looking at Brooke
once again. ''Something I've waited far too long to
say, and I hope she'll hear me out.''

With that he moved away from the dais as reluctant
applause rang out. Obviously the crowd didn't know
what to make of his brief and somewhat cryptic
speech. Neither did Brooke. But she sensed she was
about to find out when she noticed him walking de-
liberately toward her.

The fight-or-flight reflex took over and she stood,
but not before he was standing so close that she could
almost touch him. And, oh, did she want to.

''We need to talk,'' he stated without formality.

Brooke stood cemented to the spot, unsure of what
to do next. While everyone nearby turned their attention on them, Jared took her by the elbow and guided
her past the tables of gawking guests and led her to
a small waiting area near the elevators.

Once there, they faced each other, an uncomfort-
able quiet hanging over them like a stifling summer
haze. Brooke hated silence, yet she wasn't sure how
to begin. So she settled for the obvious opener.
''How's your hand?''

''Okay.'' He surveyed her face as if he was seeing
it for the first time.

Again more silence ticked off until he finally

spoke. "These past two weeks have been hell, Brooke."

She could definitely relate to that. "I know. The surgery must have been tough on you."

"Not the surgery. I can handle that. What I can't handle is having so much unresolved between us." He forked a hand through his golden hair and turned his face to the opposite wall. "I'm no good at this."

Brooke folded her arms across her waist. "Take your time. I have all the patience in the world."

"Yeah, you proved that to me from the beginning." He looked at her once again with his soulful blue eyes. "I realize that I put you in a bad position. You didn't have any choice but to let Nick handle the contracture diagnosis. I'm sorry I came down so hard on you."

This wasn't what she wanted to hear. She didn't need an apology. She needed him to say that he still wanted her, but obviously this was just a play for mercy, not a proclamation of his undying love. As if she really should have expected that. "Okay, Dr. Granger. Apology accepted. I'm sorry, too. For everything."

His blue gaze, reflecting a pain she'd never seen before, sliced her to the heart. "Are you sorry you got involved with me?"

She looked down for a moment in an attempt to regain her composure. "No. I don't think I'll ever be sorry for that. I had a great time."

"Brooke, look at me." She raised her eyes to his solemn expression. "Is that all it was, a great time?"

"You tell me."

"No, that's not all it was. At least not for me. And

I think it meant more to you, too. That's what I'm hoping.''

The pounding in Brooke's ears muffled his words. She wasn't certain she had heard correctly. "Come again?''

"I'm saying I miss you. Your smile. Your corny jokes. Even the grief you've given me over the past few weeks. Definitely your body.'' He slipped an arm around her waist and pulled her closer. She didn't have the strength of will or the desire to protest. "I'm also saying that I can't stand the thought of spending another day without you in my life.''

All her resolve headed down the hall without her, replaced by another steady stream of unsolicited tears. "Really?''

"Yeah, really.'' He kissed her damp cheek. "I love you, Brooke. I've known that for a while now, but I wasn't ready to accept it. Now I am, and I need you more than anything on God's green earth. And it's not about your expertise in the therapy department, although I have no complaints there. It's about your ability to make me feel whole again, even during the toughest times. It's the way you love *me*—the man— not the doctor.''

Now she was really crying. All she could do was sob like a lost little girl. Yet she'd never felt so secure in all her life in Jared's arms.

He thumbed away a tear from her chin with heart-rending tenderness. "Hell, I didn't mean to make you cry.''

"I'm not crying.'' A ridiculous denial. "Okay, so maybe I am crying. I seem to do a lot of that lately.''

"My fault, too, I guess.''

She sniffed. "Maybe."

"So what do you say, Brooke Lewis? Will you give this jaded man another chance?"

She smiled. "Maybe."

He touched his lips to hers. "Anything else I can do to persuade you?"

Circling her arms around his neck, she said, "A little more lip service would be nice, and not the kind that involves talking."

He studied her with mock surprise. "What? And ruin our reputations here in the hallowed halls of Memorial?"

"Mine maybe, but not yours. The masses expect nothing less from the Stud of Surgery."

He gave her a smile, then the most tender of kisses. Full of emotion, of need. The kind of need that Brooke could certainly live with. Her heart soared; her body trembled. She found true solace in the moment. *He loves me* echoed in her muddled mind. She gave no thought to their surroundings, nor did she care who might play witness to their affection. She only cared that for once in her life, she had someone in her arms who she could need without fear of losing herself completely. Someone she could love wholeheartedly, without conditions, and be loved back. About time.

"Get a room, Granger. The census is low so I'm sure you can find one quick."

Nick Kempner's abrupt request caused Jared to end the kiss, much to Brooke's dismay. Jared turned Brooke in his arms, and she leaned back against him to face his colleague.

"You know, Nick, you've got real bad timing," Jared said.

"You know, Granger, yours is looking pretty good."

Michelle chose that moment to whisk by, tossing Brooke a wave and a wily grin. "You owe me one, sis. And I expect to collect," she called out as she headed toward the stairwell.

Nick watched Michelle's progression until she slipped through the heavy metal door. "Now *that's* looking pretty good," he said, one of his espresso-colored eyes narrowed, as if he was about to take his best shot.

"I thought you gave up women for good," Jared said.

Nick grinned. "I might have to make an exception. Just this once, mind you."

Brooke smiled to herself. Maybe Nick and Michelle might mesh. Find the happiness she had found with Jared. She wanted everyone to be happy, especially her sister. "I'll be sure to mention your name," Brooke said. "But I have to warn you, Michelle's anything but easy."

Nick rubbed a hand over his shadowed jaw. "Nothing better than a good challenge."

Ignoring Nick, Jared stared down on Brooke's joyful face. He felt a certain stab of pride that he had brought back her smile. "You want to get out of here?"

She looked up at him with disappointment. "I've got a full schedule this afternoon, so I guess you'll have to wait."

"I can't wait. Not for this."

Nick released a cynical laugh. "What are you going to do now, Granger? Utilize the sofa?"

Jared glared at his friend who was in danger of losing that status if he didn't scram. "No, but I'm going to politely ask you to get out of here. I have something important to ask Brooke."

"I'm sure Brooke wouldn't mind if I hang around, would you Brooke?"

Nick's ensuing grin was a tad more lecherous than Jared cared to tolerate. Especially when it was aimed at the love of his life. "Leave, Kempner. Now."

Nick held up his palms in surrender. "Okay. I get the hint." He started down the hall but turned and pointed at Brooke. "You and me, we've got to talk. I know all his dirty secrets. I'll tell them to you if you'll give me the scoop on your sister."

"Sounds like a deal to me," Brooke said, laughter in her voice.

Nick was now out of sight, and most of the luncheon crowd had passed by, giving Jared the opportunity he needed. He turned Brooke around to face him. "I have something for you," he said, feeling more than a little self-conscious. This wasn't at all what he'd planned, but for some reason it seemed necessary to just go for it.

"Don't tell me. You stole a rose from the table," she said with a teasing smile.

"Nope. Not this time." He dropped his arms from around her and lifted them up from his sides. "It's in my pocket."

Her grin widened. "I just bet it is."

"I'm serious, Brooke. Left pocket. Find it."

"My pleasure." She reached down and rummaged

through his jacket while Jared fought impatience and the heat her touch was generating in his randy body.

He could tell the exact moment she found the surprise by the startled look on her face. Slowly she lifted the blue velvet box from his pocket and simply stared at it. Then she steepled her fingers together, the box nestled between her palms, and brought her hands to her face as if in prayer.

"Aren't you going to open it?" Jared asked. He sounded like a kid at Christmas, but he couldn't help it. He'd imagined this moment for weeks. "I'd give it a shot, but I'm afraid I'll drop it, considering my bum hand." Considering his strong case of the nerves.

"Sure." She opened the box with agonizing slowness, then peeked inside. Her dark eyes went wide. "Oh, wow."

"Well?"

She continued to gape at the emerald-cut diamond ring, her lips parted in surprise. "If this is your idea of a peace offering, then we have to fight more. And often."

He touched her cheek. "It's my idea of a marriage proposal. So what do you say? Will you marry me?"

In all his years, Jared had never seen such joy on a woman's face. He intended to spend the next fifty keeping it on Brooke's face as much as possible.

"I'll try my best to make you happy, babe," he said.

"Well, I guess if you put it that way..." She grabbed him around the neck in a voracious hug. "Of course I'll marry you. Then I can spend all my time giving you grief." She leaned back and regarded him with another shaky smile. "Would you care to put it on my finger now?"

"It might take me a while."

She tossed the box onto the nearby sofa. "I've still got an hour. Or forever, for that matter."

He fumbled with the ring and, with Brooke's help, slipped it on her left hand. It glimmered in the overhead fluorescent lights, just like her dark eyes.

She held it up. "It's beautiful, Jared."

"Yeah. As beautiful as its owner." But Brooke's beauty was far-reaching. Far beyond superficial attributes. Her beauty came from her caring soul, her quick smile, the beautiful way she loved him with all her heart—all that she had to give.

"Hope you're ready," she began, her voice slightly tremulous with unshed tears, "because I'm going to put you through the toughest workout of your life."

"I'm counting on it. Can we start tonight?"

"I meant in terms of the therapy on your hand."

"Damn."

She flashed a dimple. "When we're not doing the other kind of therapy."

"You had me worried there." Jared's smile dropped as he prepared to tie up one last loose thread. "Brooke, you and I both know I may never go back to surgery."

She brushed a kiss across his cheek. "Not if I have anything to do with it. And besides, you'll have me full-time, round the clock. Your own private slave-driver-cum-therapist."

"I can't wait." And he couldn't. Not any longer than he had to. "How about a Christmas wedding?"

"Heck, no. January. I don't want to give anyone the license to buy only one gift."

"Good thinking. And after we're married, we'll talk about that clinic you want to open."

"Right now being with you is my main goal. That and helping you recover the use of that finger." A sigh slipped out of her lips. "We still have a lot to learn about each other, don't we?"

"Yeah, but I can't think of any better way to spend my time off before I go back to work."

More pure elation in her eyes. "So you've finally come around to seeing things my way, have you? That's what I love about you, Jared Granger. You're very easy to persuade. Most of the time."

He slipped his hand underneath her lab coat and tugged her forward until they were completely touching, letting her know immediately what he had in mind for her.

"*Dr.* Granger," she said in a breathless tone. "Is that another ring in your pocket?"

"You know damned well it's not."

She looked around and then wriggled her hips. "Yes, I guess you're right. Much, much larger than a ring box."

"So *now* can I persuade you to call Macy and tell her you have plans for the afternoon?"

Brooke worried her bottom lip—after she covertly grabbed his butt underneath his jacket. "I'll tell her I've been bitten by the love bug. If you'll promise me something first."

"Anything."

"Could you use your connections to see if there's any leftover fruit from lunch? I saw a really big bowl on the table. I'd hate to think they might throw it out when we could so easily utilize it in more creative endeavors.''

"Always thinking on your feet." Jared laughed and hugged her hard. ''And that, Brooke Lewis, is what I love about you.''

* * * * *

Don't miss Dr. Nick Kempner
and Michelle Lewis's story
in the next book of Kristi Gold's
MARRYING AN M.D.
Look for DR. DESIRABLE
in February 2002!

If you enjoyed what you just read,
then we've got an offer you can't resist!

Take 2 bestselling
love stories FREE!
Plus get a FREE surprise gift!

January 2002
**THE REDEMPTION
OF JEFFERSON CADE**
#1411 by BJ James

Don't miss the fifth
book in BJ James'
exciting miniseries
featuring irresistible
heroes from Belle Terre,
South Carolina.

February 2002
THE PLAYBOY SHEIKH
#1417 by Alexandra Sellers

Alexandra Sellers
continues her sensual
miniseries about
powerful sheikhs
and the women
they're destined
to love.

March 2002
**BILLIONAIRE
BACHELORS: STONE**
#1423 by Anne Marie Winston

Bestselling author
Anne Marie Winston's
Billionaire Bachelors prove they're
not immune to the power of love.

MAN OF THE MONTH

Some men are made for lovin'—and you're sure to love
these three upcoming men of the month!

Available at your favorite retail outlet.

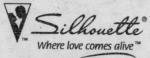

Where love comes alive™

SDMOM02Q1